SHATTERSKIN

BECA LEWIS

Published by:
Perception Publishing
https://perceptionpublishing.com

This book is a work of fiction. All characters in this book are fictional. However, as a writer, I have, of course, made some of the book's characters composites of people I have met or known.

ISBN-13: 978-0-9719529-1-1

Table of Contents

One

It was as terrifying as standing at the open door of an airplane getting ready to jump. Or at least I imagined it would feel the same way even though I had never experienced that myself. Leaning forward and seeing the ground thousands of feet away, not knowing where the wind would blow you. Not knowing what you will find when you land.

At least people jumping out of planes got to practice, and they could see the ground. Besides they have parachutes for heaven's sake.

What I was doing was completely different. No practice. No parachute. Can't see where I'm going. Just step into a void. Leaping into the unknown. No visual clues. Nothing to stop me from smashing myself to bits somewhere.

Suzanne's voice was whispering in my ear telling me to go, go, go. She was getting annoyed. She hissed at me which she had never done before. She said I was being melodramatic and it didn't suit me at all. Just go!

I understood that she was rushing me for a reason. The portal was designed to stay open only for a few brief moments. The short time frame was necessary. It was to keep the monsters that lived in each dimension from leaping into another one.

Yes, there are monsters. Aren't there always monsters? Sometimes they look like people, and sometimes they don't. But letting a monster travel to a new dimension would introduce a danger to the inhabitants of that dimension, and there was a strong chance that they wouldn't be able to defend themselves against it. It could mean the end of that world somehow.

It was like all the trees that were dying in my world. Dying because a bug, or parasite, traveled from one country to the next where there were no natural predators to stop them. One species after another of our beloved trees were leaving our earth. It was heartbreaking, but at the moment I couldn't do anything about that problem. There were too many present ones to deal with, like leaping into a portal to someplace else.

Maybe when I came back, I could help. Suzanne told me that there might be something they would find where we were going that could stop the killing of our trees. After all, her people lived in what she described as a magnificent old growth forest.

I couldn't wait to see it. I wanted it more than anything else in the world. Still, I couldn't move. I couldn't bring myself to step into the destiny that was waiting for me. Once the portal closed, it would not open again for me for a long time, if at all. Or at least that was what they told me. Sometimes I wasn't sure if anyone was telling me the whole truth about anything.

The only thing I really knew was that I was more afraid than I had ever been. All my powers were useless. They couldn't help me now. I was just an ordinary girl going on an adventure like no other, and if I didn't leap soon, I might never get to go.

I had been dreaming about doing this very thing from the moment I learned about dimension traveling. I knew it was for me. I had to go. Had to. Had to. It called me. It was in my genes. It was mine to do.

And yet, I was paralyzed.

The longer I hesitated, the harder it became. It was embarrassing. For years I had been begging to be the one that went with Suzanne to her dimension. Now she was giving me a chance, and I couldn't move.

Seconds ticked by. I felt as if I was shaking so hard that both dimensions would be experiencing an earthquake. What I was finding out was that when you are thinking about the unknown, it isn't nearly as scary as when you are actually living it. The unknown is a mysterious, and probably a dangerous, place.

Besides, what if the portal didn't work? I had heard whispered rumors that sometimes the gateway closes midstream, or diverts the traveler to somewhere they didn't mean to go. Sometimes people disappear forever. Perhaps they vanished into one of the hundreds of unexplored dimensions. Or maybe they disappeared altogether because what if there were empty places? No dimensions at all? The point is, no one knows. Or at least no one was telling me.

Those whispers happened at night when everyone thought that I was asleep. Instead, I was listening at the crack of the door to every conversation.

I never slept when there were people other than my parents and brother in the house. Sometimes I listened because I had an idea that it was my job to keep guard, even though no one had ever asked me to. Besides, guard against what? It was that unknown thing again. I wasn't afraid of monsters under the bed, or in the closet, as much as I was of what I knew to be there. I couldn't see them. I felt them.

Sometimes I wondered if I was crazy. After all, didn't crazy people see and feel things that others couldn't? Or was it what Suzanne had told me, that knowing that there are things most people are not aware of did not make one crazy. It was a matter of who believes you and what you do with the knowledge.

When she uses the word knowledge, I get all goose pimply. I love knowing things, Things people already know and things most people don't know.

That's the other reason I listen at the crack of doors. I can't stand people knowing things that I don't know. It's arrogant of me to be this way I realize. Who am I to have to know? But the fact is, I have to know.

How do things happen? How do they work? Why are they built that way? Perhaps my mom should have named me Curiosity because there is nothing I don't want to know. Even bad stuff. I have to find out. Which is why I have to be a dimension traveler. I have to find out what is on the other side.

"You only have seconds left, Hannah, it's now or maybe never," whispered Suzanne in my ear. It dawned on me that perhaps I was afraid because I didn't know how they put the portal together.

But I would never know unless I went there and found out for myself. Anyway, Suzanne is an experienced dimension traveler, and she was going with me. Wherever we went, we would be going together. There was a kind of safety in that. Or at least I pretended that there was. Sometimes pretending is the only way through a problem.

I took a deep breath and stepped in, and then I was gone.

Two

"Zonk it," I heard myself say as I tripped over something and fell flat on my face.

"Whoa, already swearing like a native. I bet that entrance will go down into the history of Erda. Kids will read about it and wonder how it was possible that the great, fantastic, Hannah from Earth fell on her face and started swearing," the voice said.

"Who the ziffer are you," I said sitting up holding my head. Perhaps I had gone crazy after all. There was no one there. No Suzanne. No one.

Besides I don't swear, those words coming out of my mouth couldn't be happening, if they were swear words. They sounded pretty weird for swearing. It was all a dream. I probably hadn't even left yet.

On the other hand, it was a pretty vivid dream. My head hurt. Zounds, it hurt. There I go again, swearing weird words, even in a dream. Mom will not be happy with me. Mom. That's it. I'll wake up, find her, and see what she is doing. I'll hug dad. I'll find my little brother Ben and tell him about my dream. Maybe I'll delay the dimension traveling until I get older. Suzanne will understand, won't she?

I pulled myself to a standing position thinking that would wake me up, but within moments I was knocked down again by something flying right at me. A flash of red was all I saw as I fell backward. Whatever it was landed directly on top of me.

So far this was one of the weirdest dreams I had ever had. Sitting on my stomach was a miniature dinosaur, or maybe a dragon of sorts. Its huge beak was positioned directly in front of my nose. Its head looked every which way, scanning the sky, the trees. Wait, sky and trees.

Until that moment I hadn't noticed that the sky was the same, but for all my love of trees, I had never seen trees that looked like these. Or at least trees that could do what these trees were doing. They were leaning towards me. Some were almost touching the ground as if they were listening.

When I turned to them, they straightened up. I swear, some of the trees even turned their back on me. Swiveled somehow. I started to curse and stopped myself just in case I was dreaming and was still the girl who lived in the Earth dimension. The thought that perhaps I had traveled to a new realm after all, occurred to me. Maybe in this one, I was different? Still me, but different somehow.

The dinosaur on top of me squawked and lifted off to land in one of the leaning trees. Seeing it fly I realized what it was, even though it didn't seem possible.

I could believe that Lady, the pileated woodpecker that had befriended me on Earth, was in my dream, but how could she have dimension traveled with me? Besides, she was so big!

"You are pretty dense," the voice said again. "But given that you smacked your head, we'll give you a break. For now."

Holding my head, I stood and looked around. I was in a clearing, surrounded by trees—a blue sky above me and what appeared as a meadow of sorts in front of me. I recognized some of the flowers, even though they were not quite right, somehow. That mystery would have to be solved later.

For now, I needed to figure out where I was and what I was supposed to do next.

If I did dimension travel, where was Suzanne? If there had been a portal, it was no longer there. Stumbling to a nearby rock, still holding my head, I sat down hoping to gain some perspective.

What was I supposed to do? Where was I supposed to go? Why was Lady here with me, but not Suzanne? And who spoke to me?

The rock moved, or slid, and then stopped. *This is what going crazy feels like,* I thought. Besides, I'm hungry. Why didn't I think to bring food?

I knew why. I thought Suzanne would be with me. She would show me the ropes, explain the mysteries of her dimension, her realm. Take me to her friends. I would visit, and then I could go home.

"I'm afraid that going home is not possible, Hannah," I heard Suzanne say from somewhere behind me.

I turned to see her standing by one of the trees that had been leaning towards me but was now standing as straight and rigid as any tree on Earth. I wouldn't have known that it was Suzanne though. I had never seen her as a solid being before.

She had always visited us as a wisp of a person, sometimes as transparent as a mist, other times more substantial but with a body that trailed off, that looked like what some people called ghosts but without the white sheet.

I knew that my mother had met Suzanne as a human person before she had begun to dimension travel and I had seen pictures of Suzanne. She had been beautiful. She still was, but not the same. First, because she wasn't wearing what she had when we stepped into the portal.

"You don't like what I'm wearing?" the person who looked like Suzanne said. If it was Suzanne, she had transformed her flowing white and black cloak with streaks of red into more practical black leggings and a red tunic type top. Her long white hair was now short, snipped into spikes.

Like a tongue-tied teenager who knew nothing, I gaped at her. "What are you?"

Her answer was to completely disappear as Lady swooped down from the top of the tree to land on the rock I had vacated after it had started to slide.

Lady cawed at me and started off into the forest. When I didn't move, she flew back and grabbed my hair.

"Ow-ziffer. Stop it. Okay, I'll follow you. But will Suzanne know where we are going?"

Once again I heard laughter, more than one kind of laughter this time. It was a chorus of laughter. I spun around. The leaves of the trees were trembling. Were they laughing at me?

I had no choice. I had to follow. But in my heart, I was scared and angry. Whoever was laughing had no right to laugh. I had been deserted. And what did Suzanne, or that woman pretending to be Suzanne, mean when she said I couldn't go home?

How dare she leave me all alone. All I had was a crazy bird. And laughing trees and a rock that didn't act like a rock.

Perhaps this is a dream after all, and I would wake up soon, but in the meantime, I needed to know what was happening. That was my thing. after all. Didn't mean I wasn't still angry, though.

Three

Still holding my head, I started to follow the bird that looked like Lady into the forest until I realized what I was doing. I was following something into somewhere without questioning what was happening. It was like getting into a strange car with an unknown person. Would I ever do that? No. Even if the person looked like someone that I knew? Well, perhaps. But birds look almost alike, don't they? So it wasn't as if I could tell Lady from another bird just like her.

Almost too late I saw the bird fly back towards me, bent on either knocking me over again or pulling my hair. Either way, I wasn't going to let that happen. I dropped to the ground and curled into a little ball and stayed there.

Probably looked pretty stupid, but at least I didn't get my hair pulled. I lifted my head just a bit and saw the bird sitting on the ground in front of me. I got the distinct impression that she was not happy with me for thinking that she looked the same as other pileated woodpeckers that looked like dinosaurs or dragons.

Birds, animals, insects could tell the difference between each other, why couldn't I? She turned her face sideways and looked directly into my eyes. Something about those eyes were familiar, and at that moment I knew for sure that it was Lady from Earth who was sitting there. I reached out to touch her head, and she pulled her head back and gave me a look that I wouldn't forget. No touching. "Okay, okay. So you're Lady. Now, what is this place?"

I took a big breath in and smelled the woods. It smelled like the forests back home. Loamy, cool, a city of insects and animals mostly invisible unless you lived there and learned to see. Before stepping into the portal, I had been learning a little about the forest behind our house. Learning more about this forest was going to be fun. Maybe it would give me a clue as to where I was, assuming I wasn't dreaming. Didn't that voice say, *Erda?*

Screwing up my courage, I decided it was time to explore. I stood up, and for the first time since I tripped and fell on my face, I looked down at myself and screamed.

Who was this person? Was it me? What looked like my hands felt the clothes that I had on. They were not what I was wearing when I was standing in the door of the portal. I had been wearing what I always wear, like most girls my age: skinny jeans, t-shirt, and at the last minute I had grabbed my favorite soft sweater.

Suzanne had told me I couldn't bring anything other than what I was wearing through the portal. Everything else would dissolve in the transfer. What I needed would be provided for me.

What she had neglected to tell me was that I would arrive in different clothes. I ran my hands over whatever it was that was covering my legs. They felt almost like the leggings I wore in the winter and looked like the ones that woman by the tree had been wearing.

However, they felt completely different from anything I had worn before. These leggings were still soft like winter leggings, but much stronger. They were as tight as my skin but so lightweight that if I hadn't seen that I was wearing them, I would have thought I had nothing on. Scary thought, that. The shirt was the same material as the leggings. Close to my body, but soft and comfortable.

As a reader of strange stories, I wondered if I was caught up in a dream, like in one of my books. Ones where people ended up in bodies that weren't theirs. Because not only were the clothes weird, so was I. Older. Not twelve anymore. The tight clothing proved that. Not me. At least not the me that lived on Earth.

"Well, you always said you were older than your Earth age, little one," the taunting voice I had first heard said. "You were right about that anyway. Everything else, well, we'll see."

"Not going anywhere until you show yourself, and explain what's happening," I answered and sat down in a huff. The strange body and clothing would have to wait. Maybe I didn't look like me, but I felt like me. That would have to be enough for now.

As I sat down, I ended up on a rock again, even though I had not noticed it. Where did it come from? Was it a rock? It looked like one. At the moment I had more pressing problems than figuring out if it was a rock, or how it got behind me, because the laughter started again. I stood, hands clenched at my side. I was sick of the taunting, and the not knowing.

"She is kinda pretty when she's angry isn't she?"

"Humph. For a human I guess."

"Human? Pretty? What the ziffer? Who are you? Come out now and show yourself," I demanded. I was too angry to demand to know where all the z swear words were coming from. It was just one more strange thing going on.

"Or else? What are you going to do, little one? Fight? You

haven't seen us yet. You don't have the advantage in this. If I were you, and luckily I'm not, I would shut up and do what you're told to do.

"This is our world, not yours."

With those words, everything stopped. It was as if everything around me sucked in a breath of air and held it, waiting for something terrible to happen.

The ground shook. Lady flew beside me and sat there, cocking her head, looking for danger.

The release of the breath was a wind so intense I had to grab a branch of a tree that happened to be nearby to keep from following the leaves and bits of things I had never seen before that were blowing past me.

"Sorry, sorry, so sorry. I'll not do it again," squeaked the voice that was taunting me seconds before.

"You're right. You won't," roared the wind. "Now show yourself to her and do your job. Take care of her!"

Four

What happened next scared me so much I thought that my hair might pop out of my head. Like quills. You know, porcupines. Maybe they did, because I shut my eyes so fast I wouldn't have seen it happen. That confirmed it. Basically, I'm a coward.

I guess I was harboring a belief that I was some kind of hotshot because on earth I had gifts. Gifts people called paranormal. Here, so far, I had nothing. Things were happening that I had no control over. Including swearing strange words and wearing clothes that looked like they belonged to some cat woman. I was no longer a little girl. I thought that would be cool. I was wrong.

So far this traveling to another dimension was turning out to be something I wished I had never decided to do. Nothing about it was fun. At all.

After cowering behind my hands for a few moments, I took a peek between my fingers. Yep. They were still there. Two of them. What they were, I wasn't sure. It would require me to look at them.

When no one shoved anything at me or ran me over, or even spoke mean words, I gathered up a tiny bit of courage and opened one eye. Supposedly keeping the other eye shut would make me safer?

I opened, closed, opened, closed, but nothing changed. They were still there. Not moving and not smiling either. One of them had a face that reminded me of a piece of bark. The other one was standing behind it, so I could only see a tiny hand and foot.

Perhaps the tiny one was afraid of me. That thought emboldened me enough to open both my eyes while taking the miniature precaution of stepping back and trying to hide behind Lady. She wasn't there. Again. She had deserted me. Nice.

It felt as if an eternity passed while I stared at two little, maybe people, standing in front of me. They stared back at me before the grumpy, bark faced one cleared its throat and said, "Sorry, sorry, so sorry." The taunter.

Now I had to decide. Was I going to taunt back, or make friends?

I took a quick look around me. No friends. Right. Could use a few. I gathered up the remnant of what had passed as courage just the day before and demanded with great authority, "Who are you?"

The thought cloud over grumpy's head was almost visible. He thought I was a joke. He was right. But the voice that came with the wind told him to take care of me. Wait. What kind of "take care of?" It must be the other kind because if it were to get rid of me, it would have been as easy as flicking a finger and I probably would have died of fright.

Instead, he just stood there like a lump of wood. He even looked like wood. Like a stump of wood with arms and legs covered in some weird green material that almost made him look like an elf. Almost. He was too wide and gnarly. He didn't fit my version of an elf anyway.

The head that belonged to the tiny hands and feet popped out behind grumpy and smiled at me. It was a real smile. I couldn't help myself. I had to smile back. I doubted if the two of them were related.

This one had a face as smooth and open as a rose petal. She stepped forward and extended a hand. Upside down. Did she want to shake hands, or was I supposed to kiss it?

She laughed and said, "Like this," as she put her hand out and Mr. Wood Face covered it with his hand sliding them off of each other like a handshake from the seventies. I expected them to wiggle their fingers after that, but maybe they didn't know that part. Or Wood Head's fingers didn't move.

I extended my hand, and she covered it. We slid back, and I wiggled my fingers.

Flower Girl laughed, and Wood Head said, "Humpf."

"I'm Hannah," I said, and then pointing at where Lady had just flown, "and that's Lady somewhere out there."

"Oh, we know who you are Earth person," Woody said. "We are supposed to get you to where you are going."

"Could we at least start with names? And then you could tell me where I am and then where we are going. And why."

When Grumpy Wood Face grunted, Flower Girl cuffed him on the back of his head. "Cut it out, Frank."

I didn't hear what she said next because I started laughing so hard I couldn't breathe. Frank? Not something exciting or even appropriate to what he looked like? Frank?

"Sorry, sorry, so sorry," I said parroting Grumpy Wood Head who was really Frank. It was too much. Who could be afraid of a Frank? The laughter felt good to me, but when I looked at my two new friends, I was embarrassed.

Frank had turned his back to me, and little Flower Girl had her arm around his back whispering something.

"No really, I am sorry. That was so mean. I think it was a release from all of this."

When they turned around I could see that they weren't sad, they were laughing, too.

"It's a joke? Is he not Frank? Or what?"

"No, we're sorry." Flower Girl said. "We've been teasing you all along. No, his name isn't Frank. He is Ruta, and my name is Beru. Ruta doesn't like change much, and you are bringing it. Me, I love it. Which is probably why we were both chosen to guide you."

"Ruta and Beru suit you both. But I don't know anything. Who chose you? And where are you taking me?"

Beru answered me. "It's best you find out as we travel. We've stayed too long here. Some powers don't want you here. We tried to do our best to keep it a secret, but by now it will be known that a portal opened, and you have returned. We have a long journey ahead of us."

"Returned? I can't have returned. I've never been here."

Beru and Ruta exchanged glances. "Perhaps we have said too much," Beru said.

I screamed as a gut-wrenching shrieking sound in the distance made the ground beneath my feet jump.

"Go now," Ruta grunted and headed into the forest. He didn't need to tell me twice. I wasn't interested in meeting whatever caused that sound. I had heard about sonic booms. Maybe that's what this was, except it was pitched so high it sounded like a giant scratching his fingernails across the sky.

It wasn't courage that had me following a lump of wood and a flower into the forest. It was fear.

Five

Ruta moved through the woods faster than I thought possible. Beru was even quicker. She kept circling back behind me and then running ahead of Ruta, and then coming back to me. I was running faster than I had ever run before, so how she was doing that was a mystery.

There was no path as far as I could see. Ruta and Beru just ran, and things moved out of their way. Or at least I thought that was what was happening. I didn't see any movement. Instead, there was an opening wherever Ruta went, and I followed Ruta through it.

After what felt like two days but was probably less than an hour, I couldn't run anymore. I tripped over my foot and fell flat on my face again for the second time in one day. I hoped it would be the last. Ruta had kept on running, but the next time Beru circled back she found me lying on the ground trying to breathe.

She clicked her fingers together, and a moment later Ruta was there.

"I don't think she can go on right now, Ruta. Let's stay here. We're far enough from the clearing, and we can hide here until Hannah rests. Your friend has told us how much energy it takes to come through that portal. You need to rest."

When Ruta turned his grumpy stern face to me, I burst into tears as I mumbled, "Thank you Beru, and I'm sorry, Ruta."

I caught a look pass between them, and I swear I saw Ruta's block face soften. I was too tired to ask what friend they were talking about.

When Beru placed a mound of leaves under my head and covered me with some mysterious cloth she pulled out of her pocket, I fell asleep within seconds. The last thing I heard before entering emptiness was Suzanne's voice saying it was safe, for now. That was enough for me. Suzanne hadn't deserted me.

****

I woke up lying on my back gazing up at a sky filled with stars. I didn't remember falling asleep in a clearing. In fact, I was sure that we were deep into a forest when we stopped. But those stars sure looked good to me. They looked just like the stars I would see when I lay on my back in our backyard. I'm not good with naming stars, but I did recognize the Big Dipper. It was a comfort to know that I was still on Earth, even though they called it Erda. It looked like home.

Home. My mom, Ben, my dad, and my friends Johnny and Sarah. I missed them all so much, and I had only been gone a day. How was I going to survive this?

When we had talked about dimension traveling, Johnny and Sarah were supposed to come with me. At least I had planned it that way. Johnny and I would discover the mysteries of this new dimension together with Sarah watching over us to make sure all was well, just like she always did.

Sarah was the wise woman everyone went to in my hometown when they had questions about something or a problem they couldn't solve. Perhaps she knew how to help because she was older. But then I knew old people who weren't so wise.

Sarah was going to come with us because her husband, Leif, had traveled to this dimension a few years before and had stayed. She wanted to be with him, so I had envisioned that for the most part, I would have Johnny all to myself.

It didn't work out that way at all. Right after I was given the green light to dimension travel, I learned that Johnny had to stay behind. He was needed where he was. Because I believed I wouldn't be gone long, I rationalized that it might work out for the best. He would miss me, and I would grow up enough for him to stop thinking of me as a little girl.

Now that I was in the middle of some strange forest with two weird little people and Suzanne had told me that I couldn't go home for a long time, I realized how stupid that romantic notion had been.

As for Sarah, the woman who wanted to be with her husband, well, she didn't come either. I didn't know she wasn't going through the portal with me. She was standing beside me as if she was coming.

At the very last moment, Sarah had stepped away whispering that she would meet me there. I started to ask how she was going to do that when Suzanne began to yell go, go, at me and I leaped in trusting all would be well.

Sure. All was well. I lay there now in a well of self-pity for a few moments until I realized that I was hungry and I smelled something cooking.

I sat up and saw Suzanne sitting cross-legged in front of a fire along with Ruta and Beru. Ruta looked very uncomfortable.

That was something I could understand. If I looked like a stump, I would not be comfortable around a fire either. On the other hand, I had no idea what a comfortable Ruta would look like. Neither of my two guides appeared to be eating.

It was Suzanne who was eating. She was holding what looked like a monster mushroom wrapped in leaves and happily taking huge bites out of it.

She looked at me and gestured at another mushroom waiting by the fire. I took it to mean it was mine and wasted no time in reaching for it. As my hand touched the food, I remembered my manners and asked Ruta and Beru if it was for them. The faces they made assured me that it wasn't.

It was most likely because I was so hungry that the wrap was the most delicious thing I ever ate. While munching away on it, I asked Ruta and Beru what they would eat. They mumbled an answer. Instead of asking what they said, I let it go. I'd find out soon enough. Now I needed to know about the shriek I had heard earlier, and where we were going. If I was going to be afraid, at least I should know what was scaring me.

"Oh. Not necessarily," Beru said.

"Not necessarily what?" I asked.

"Sometimes knowing is even more frightening. And in this case. I think that might be true."

Wow. Beru read my mind. I used to be able to do that. I wondered if it would come back to me. I looked at Ruta and Suzanne for confirmation. Suzanne nodded in agreement with Beru's words.

Oh, zounds! What had I gotten myself into?

Six

Suzanne with the spiky hair, leggings, and red tunic smiled at me, and I could feel my blood pressure going down. I had seen her do this before when my Earth friends and I were afraid. She would appear out of nowhere, and we would immediately feel calmer and prepared to face whatever danger was in front of us.

I had no idea how she did it. I knew it was one of her many abilities, most of which I hadn't seen yet. Seeing her smile, and feeling the result, made me wonder if she was the Suzanne I knew.

Or was the Suzanne I met in the Earth dimension another Suzanne, or an illusion? Could there be two of her? Could there be two of me? How did that work?

It didn't surprise me that Suzanne knew what I was thinking. What surprised me was that she decided to answer my unspoken question.

"Dimension traveling is tricky. You might find another version of yourself when you enter a dimension because most dimensions are the same with only slight variations.

"On the other hand, if the person you are has already died in the dimension you are traveling to, you would not meet yourself. On top of that, not everyone exists in every dimension. However, you never know until you arrive if the being that is you also exists there.

"Think of all the trillions of decisions made each day that could spin a universe off into a new future. If your parents never met, you would most likely not show up in that dimension."

"What do you mean, 'most likely?'" I asked Suzanne.

"Just that. No one knows precisely how this works. The thing to remember is that if something happens in one dimension, it is possible that it happens in another one, but in a different way."

"Since there is a Ruta and a Beru in Erda, a version of them could also exist in what we call the Earth?" I asked.

"This one's easy, because I know there is. I've met them."

I took a moment to ponder that. If Suzanne had met them, had I?

The Earth that I had left less than a day ago had already started to feel more like a dream than a reality. Is that how it worked? Maybe it was designed that way to keep people from moving back and forth between dimensions unwittingly causing havoc.

If where you came from started to feel more like a dream, it forced you into being present. If you forgot that you had lived somewhere else before, or thought it was a dream, then the desire to return wouldn't be there, or it would fade away.

On the other hand, maybe some people never forgot. That would be me.

I had no intention of forgetting. I would get back to the Earth dimension someday. Not just to see my parents, but also to see Johnny. I reached over and felt my left wrist. The day before I left, Johnny had given me a friendship bracelet. One of those bracelets that you make yourself with yarn. He thought it would stay with me just like my clothes would and he was right. It was a promise that we would find each other again.

Perhaps Johnny thought of it just as friends, but I knew it was more. Or at least it could be someday.

Everyone was staring at me. Hopefully, they didn't know what I was thinking. Besides, I needed to concentrate on learning about the world I was living in now.

"What about you?" I asked Suzanne. "So if you aren't an illusion in either dimension, are there two of you? Or do you only look different here?"

"I look different here because here I look like myself. But there is only one of me, just as there is only one of you. At least in the two dimensions we are talking about, Earth and Erda, and a few other ones that I have visited. We do have people living in Erda who have traveled more widely than I have, and I've been told that it is true wherever they have been."

"Wait, are you telling me that people here know who I am, and look for other versions of me when they travel to different dimensions? What does that mean? What dimension do I belong in then?"

"That's something you'll be discovering soon," Suzanne said. "For now it's enough to know that sometimes people move to a dimension which is not their home and..."

Suzanne was ready to tell me more when the shriek we heard earlier sounded again. It not only shook the earth, it felt as if it sucked air up and away if just for a moment. Whatever it was, it knew exactly how to scare the ziffer out of me. Apparently, everyone else was afraid too, because within seconds Suzanne, Ruta, and Beru were on their feet.

Beru swept out her hand, and all traces of the fire vanished. Another swipe and all the trees were back in place. I gasped at what I had seen but had no time to process it. I was pushed forward by Suzanne, her hand feeling like a claw on my back. Once again, I heard her whisper, "Go, go, go." This time, I knew that pausing to decide was not a good idea. I ran, and once again Suzanne disappeared. I had no time to wonder where she went. I just hoped she was safe.

Seven

"Open up, Hannah," Beru urged me as we ran. "Accept the help that is being offered to you. Breathe it in."

I was panting so hard I had no breath to ask her what she meant by help. I was nearing my last ounce of energy, and neither Beru nor Ruta seemed tired at all. They definitely knew something I didn't know.

"You don't know what I am talking about?" Beru asked.

Up ahead I heard Ruta snort in derision. He was right. I was more than useless. I shook my head. No, I didn't know what they were talking about.

"Feel it, Hannah, just as you did before you came here. Feel the forest. Feel the ground beneath your feet. Feel what they have to give you. Reach out. Let them in." Then Beru, sweet little Beru with the beautiful face, yelled at me, "Do it. Do it now!"

I gasped in surprise and felt a bolt of energy rush in. I was no longer running on my own. I was moving with the forest, not through it.

I don't know how long we ran. I lost all sense of time and surroundings. The forest around me blurred into a tunnel of green that flowed back the way we had come. In front of me,

I could see Ruta moving, no, gliding, almost as if he wasn't moving his legs at all. Behind me, I could feel Beru's eyes effortlessly pushing me forward. There was no need for her to run forward and back to check on me. The three of us moved as one. It was glorious. I wanted it to last forever.

How much time passed I don't know, and although I had no idea where we were, I could tell that we were moving upward.

Eventually, the world slowed down as we stopped running and began to walk instead. We were on a path. Not one created by Ruta moving through the woods, clearing the way. This path was like many of the trails my dad and I used to hike together in the mountains near our home. If I wasn't walking with Ruta and Beru, I might have thought I was home again.

That notion was blasted from my mind as we crested a hill, and I saw what appeared to be a castle. Not what I expected at all. On the other hand, what was I expecting? If I was truthful with myself, I was hoping we were going to see Suzanne's people, the Forest Circle, and I said as much to Ruta and Beru.

"Shh…," hissed Ruta. "Are you crazy?"

At first, I was dumbstruck to hear Ruta say more than one word. Maybe he didn't often talk because his voice did not match his appearance. Unless he was hollow, because that's what he sounded like: a hollow stump.

When his block face darkened, I realized he could probably read my mind, and I was in trouble. What had happened to me? I didn't usually think things like that about people. Or did I and I hadn't noticed? My whole world was flipping upside down.

"Ziffer it," Ruta said.

"Ziffer it? Are you swearing? Do you mean zipper it? Well, that I can understand, I think," I babbled. "After all we were running from something, and maybe you want me to be quiet?"

"No," Ruta rumbled. "I meant ziffer it. Zonk you. Zounds,

how did we get the assignment anyway?"

It was horrible. I started laughing again. "Seriously, what's with the z words?"

Ruta just stared at me as if he wanted to take his whole body and club me with it. I tried arranging my face to look like his when Beru stepped in.

"Stop it you two. Especially you, Hannah. Didn't you learn any manners? Did you treat people that didn't look like you differently in your realm? Ruta is protecting you, and you are rude and ungrateful. Aren't you ashamed of yourself?"

Yes, I was ashamed of myself. But it was because when the magic I had experienced while running stopped, I felt so much fear I wanted to crawl inside the nearest hole and never come out again.

It wasn't just fear for what I didn't know or for myself. It was a weight of fear that fell on me like a blanket. Smothering me. I have been afraid before, but nothing like what I was feeling then. I was covering it up with rudeness.

Beru looked at me with such sadness in her eyes I thought that perhaps she understood. But Lady's arrival halted all conversation. She swooped over our heads and headed in the direction of the castle. The meaning was clear. Follow.

We didn't run. We ambled. I didn't think we would ever get there. Ruta and Beru took turns switching us in and out of the trees. We'd stop, and Beru would put her finger to her lips to tell me not to talk. That was okay. I had nothing more to say. The stopping was driving me crazy, though.

After perhaps the tenth stop, Beru must have sensed my frustration and whispered in my ear, "We're listening."

Her finger on my mouth told me not to ask what they were listening for, so I thought I would try listening too. I heard nothing. Nothing? How could there be no sounds in the forest?

Where were the bird songs, the rustling of leaves in the wind, the millions of insects that thrived in forests?

It was impossible for them not to be here. I know that every creature in the forest makes it thrive. Eliminate one, and everyone suffers. If the forest wasn't working, then the trees would be dying, and they weren't. The only explanation I had was that everything was being quiet on purpose. Either that or I had gone deaf.

After another million stops to listen, I heard something. At first, it was far away. Then it started to move closer. Like a train whistle heard in the distance and becoming louder as the train moves forward.

But this sound moved by itself. If it were music, it would sound like a hundred notes harmonizing together. As it got louder and louder, Beru and Ruta looked at each other before each of them reached for one of my hands. By then they had to pry them off my ears the sound was so loud.

As our hands touched, the note landed directly on top of us. It wrapped itself around us and picked us up into the air so that we were hovering over the treetops. It was as if the note had created a clear bubble and put us inside of it. Inside, it was quieter than anything I had ever experienced before.

The bubble paused and then began to move back in the direction the note had come. I was glad we were moving so quickly because it meant I couldn't see anything. Heights had not been my favorite thing, but this ride was so peaceful I started to enjoy it.

Ruta and Beru continued to hold my hand. Ruta did not appear to be enjoying the ride, while Beru looked as if she was in seventh heaven.

I had only had time to think it felt like an elevator going sideways before the sound bubble descended, and dissolved, leaving us standing on the ground in front of the Castle I had seen in the distance.

A wall of beings of all sizes and shapes stood in front of the Castle. I hoped that they were friendly because they all held what appeared to be a variety of strange weapons. I guessed they were weapons even though I only recognized a few of the shapes. No one looked happy to see us. Except one. Suzanne.

Zounds, I was I glad to see her. She bowed to Ruta and Beru and motioned me forward. Holding my hand, she presented me to the crowd. Reluctantly they bowed. To me. With Suzanne's arm around my waist, she pushed me to bow back. I had no idea what was going on. The world had gone mad. Or I had. That was almost easier to accept.

Eight

"Be still," Suzanne whispered. "Do what I tell you to do, and don't act so confused. And for zounds sake, don't look around like a tourist."

I did what Suzanne told me to do. I bowed in all four directions. I tried not to look anywhere. All I could see anyway was that we were in an open courtyard in front of the Castle. As I bowed, I tried to look at our surroundings, but a blue haze blocked from my view whatever was past the Castle.

After all the bowing, Suzanne walked towards two doors leading into the Castle. Black and huge, they seemed too tall and much too heavy to open. She kept poking me with her finger to let me know that I was supposed to be walking side by side with her towards those doors.

Ruta and Beru trailed behind us. I barely knew the two of them, and Ruta had been a big grouch, but still, I felt embarrassed for them that they had to walk behind us.

"Hold your head up, Hannah. Up, up," Suzanne hissed at me.

I lifted my head, looking straight ahead as I was told to do. I couldn't believe Suzanne was having such a hissy fit. I had never seen her behave that way. Maybe on Earth she pretended to be polite, and now she was showing her true colors? I tried not to roll my eyes at her behavior.

As much as I didn't like being told what to do, I had to believe that she was trying to protect me from something. Maybe from all those beings that didn't look all that happy to see me.

I didn't have much time to look at the crowd, but most of them didn't look human, at least Earth human. The only thing they seemed to have in common was the look they gave me. What was everyone so angry about, anyway? Why did they bow to me? What had I done to deserve either treatment?

Moments later we reached the doors which silently slide sideways, and we stepped into the Castle.

Some people like the idea of castles, kings and queens and luxury. Not me. In all the pictures I have ever seen of them they looked cold and damp. I imagined musty smells and spiders in corners. Plus all those rules and regulations that royalty had to put up with didn't appeal to me at all.

So it was a pleasant surprise to discover that the inside of this castle didn't match my predetermined idea of what castles looked like.

We were standing in a beautiful garden. On either side of us, the walls rose up at least four stories high. Clear glass encased each floor making it possible to look at the stone hallways as they traveled around each level.

The atrium was as big as a football field, planted with flowers, bushes, and trees that reached almost to the fourth floor. A glass roof let in the daylight. I could see the blue sky and white clouds floating across it.

It was lovely and peaceful. But most wonderful of all, it felt familiar. The air was warm and sweet smelling just like Sarah's garden back home.

Suzanne led us down a pathway to the center of the garden. I could see a table set with five place settings. Did that mean we were going to eat? I was starving. The mushroom wrap was delicious, but that could have been days ago. I had lost all track of time.

Five places? There were only four of us. That's when I saw him.

****

For all I knew, he had been there all along because as he started towards us, he made not one sound. His face gave me no clue if he was friendly or not. That is, until Suzanne rushed forward and fell into his arms.

He stepped back holding her at arm's length. His face that a moment before looked like a constipated storm cloud, was beaming at her.

Suzanne turned to me and said, "Dad, this is …"

"I know who she is," he boomed. "Hannah, welcome home. I hope you have enjoyed your journey because it is only going to get harder after this."

Dad? Home? What the zonk?

The only dad I knew Suzanne had was someone named Earl. The giver of the stones, the head of the Forest Circle. Could this be Earl? No one told me he was a giant that moved like the wind.

"Well, I wasn't that on Earth was I, little one? And my name's not Earl here, just as yours is not Hannah."

"Not now, dad," Suzanne said laying her hand on his arm. The man I knew as Earl smiled at her and then at me and said, "Okay, it's Hannah and Earl for now."

Suzanne hooked her arm around Earl's as they walked to the

table and I followed obediently. Inside I was screaming to know what was going on.

It took a lot of effort to push aside my impatience and choose to watch and wait. Someone would tell me what was happening at some point. At first, I hoped it would be soon, and then changed my mind. Maybe this was another time that not knowing was better than knowing.

My wish to be ignorant wasn't granted though, because Beru decided to tell me. Not then. Later. Much later. First, we ate.

Beru and Ruta sat on chairs which reminded me of baby high chairs. At least I was wise enough not to mention it, although that could have been not so much me being wise as being distracted by the things that brought in our food.

Our table was situated beside a transparent wall that within seconds contained what looked like metal toadstools carrying platters of food attached to their heads. When another toadstool popped up seconds later, I saw that the wall was an elevator. The doors slid open, and the five toadstools slid forward.

"Dad, I thought we talked about this."

"They're not on the grid, daughter. Each one operates separately, and they only do this one function. There is nothing to worry about."

Suzanne gave her dad a look of impatience, but then sighed and let it go.

The metal toadstools arranged themselves by each of our chairs so we could serve ourselves what we wanted from the tray on their head.

Most of the food looked familiar, but I tasted everything even if I didn't know what I was eating. It was all delicious. No one spoke.

The only sound was the clinking of our silverware and the various forms of chewing. Chewing is not my favorite sound, but there was no way I was going to break the silence by talking.

By the time we had finished eating, the familiar stars were becoming visible in the sky. It was my second night in Erda, and I still knew nothing.

"No questions, Hannah?" Earl asked.

"Other than everything? What is this place, who are you really, what am I doing here? You mean other than those questions?"

Earl laughed, and a breeze danced around the table.

"You're here to train."

"Train? For what?"

Earl looked at Suzanne and said, "She doesn't know?"

"Know what?" I demanded.

"This world, our kingdom, is in trouble. You are here to help save it," Earl answered.

"Save it?" I squeaked. "Me?"

"You. Training begins tomorrow. Better get some rest. You are going to need it." Earl said.

He pushed back from the table, stood, and pointed to a door that I hadn't noticed before. "Through that door, your future awaits. Don't disappoint me."

I stared at him as he left as silently as he arrived. First, he was there, and then he wasn't, and he never answered the question: How was I going to save a kingdom?

Nine

I decided that Earl must have actually been present. I had seen him eat the food. Obviously this effortless coming and going was different than remote viewing, or astral projection in my world.

Earl was actually present rather than a projection. Was this ability something I would learn? Did I want to? What did they mean by training? I kept staring where Earl had gone, expecting him to reappear, and tell me more. Someone had to explain to me what was happening.

"Why didn't you tell me what I am supposed to do here?" I demanded of Suzanne. "You know I can't save a kingdom."

Suzanne stood and looked down at me. I swear her tunic blazed red as she answered through clenched teeth. "You can, and you will. Even if it kills all of us, including you, this world must survive. Do what my father told you to do. Get rest."

She looked at Beru. "Take her to her room and make sure she stays there. You know where to bring her tomorrow. Ruta, you're with me."

This was not at all what I thought I was coming to this dimension for, and now that I was here, I realized it was the last place I wanted to be. Dimension traveling was supposed to be fun and exciting. What was happening to me wasn't either of those two things.

I liked Suzanne on Earth. Here she scared the ziffer out of me. Either I needed to wake up from this nightmare or go home. Someone had to take me back. I didn't realize that I was crying until Beru dabbed at my face with a napkin.

"I don't understand, Beru. What are they talking about? What are they going to train me to do? What am I going to learn?"

"Fighting and magic," she answered. "One you know, one you don't."

"I don't know either," I said, now openly sobbing.

"And that's where you're wrong. Don't make me use my magic to get you moving. You won't like it."

"What won't I like, Beru? Your magic or your fighting."

"You won't like either. Good thing for you, I am on your side. Even if I hadn't been ordered to stay with you, I will. I will be with you no matter what, because my people are counting on you. All of the inhabitants of this world are counting on you."

"Nothing like making a girl feel welcome," I mumbled as I followed her as she headed for another door off of the atrium. I hadn't noticed all the doors before. How would I remember which ones to go through? Where did they all go to anyway?

"Okay. Here's your first training," Beru said, stopping beside a fern that grew higher than my head. "Close your eyes. Say to yourself, 'I see these doors. I know these doors.' Keep saying that. Feel it. Reach out in your imagination and feel yourself inside the essence of the door. Let yourself know the door."

This was the training? Stupid, but not so hard. I closed my eyes and tried to do what she was telling me. Saying the words was easy, feeling the doors, not so much. How could I feel the doors? How could I know the doors? I heard Beru say that we were not moving until I experienced the doors. It made me angry.

She hissed at me, “Feel the doors. Do it. Do it. Do it.”

I got angrier. Beru kept prodding me until I was so mad I thought I would burst.

“Use it, Hannah. Turn the anger into wanting to know the door and feel its essence.”

At first, the anger just kept growing and I could feel it eating away at me. It scared me. It scared me enough that I decided to do what Beru had said. I imagined turning the anger around to serve me instead of hurting me. I used all the emotion the anger had created to know the door.

Then magically all of the anger vanished, and I knew. “Open your eyes, Hannah, and look at the doors.”

When I opened my eyes, I saw the doors differently. Each one was unique, and each one had a faintly glowing number on it. But I didn't need to look with my eyes. I had already seen the doors in their true essence. I knew each door personally.

“Why the numbers?” I asked.

“The numbers are there just in case you need to call their name, but the numbers can't be seen unless you've opened your mind to see them. Good job, Hannah.”

I basked in the glow of her praise. For the first time since leaving home, I felt hopeful. Knowing the doors had felt wonderful. It would be amazing to know other things like that too.

We walked through the door marked with a number three and headed down a dimly lit hallway. The low light wasn't scary. It was comforting. I wondered if the lights would be brighter during the day. Not that I could see any lighting fixtures.

The entire hallway was the light, including the ceiling, even though it looked like stone. I didn't understand how that could be, but there it was.

We turned a corner, and I saw another door at the end of that hallway. I knew it was my door, my room. I imagined a soft, cozy bed and realized that I was exhausted. A good night's sleep and more training to know things in the morning, and maybe all of this wouldn't be so bad.

"Will all my training be like that?" I asked.

Beru turned to look at me, and I could see the sadness in her eyes. "No. That didn't hurt."

With that cheerful note, she opened the door to my room and after I walked in, locked it behind me.

Ten

When the lock clicked, my first instinct was to cry out and beat my fists on the door so Beru would open it again. But now that I had felt the life of a door, it didn't seem like something I wanted to do anymore. I wasn't sure if beating on them would hurt them. I knew it would hurt me.

Besides, I was so tired my eyes were barely open. All I could focus on was the big cozy looking bed waiting for me. I chose to let the fact that I had been locked in not bother me, for now.

What felt like only minutes later, the door opened and Beru, looking fresh and rested, was at my bedside shaking me. "Get up, lazy bones. Your first trainer is waiting for you, and she hates to be kept waiting. You have five minutes to get ready. Go."

"Bossy, bossy," I mumbled as I stumbled into what I could see was a bathroom. Everything I could need in a bathroom was waiting for me. I brushed by teeth, splashed water on my face, found something I thought might be face cream and put it on my face, and brushed my hair back into a ponytail.

There was no mirror to check what I looked like. I assumed that was on purpose. Looking down on a different body was freaky enough. They probably didn't want me to see my new face.

"That's not the reason," Beru said as I came out of the bathroom.

"What's not the reason?" I asked.

"Why there isn't a mirror in your room. You won't find any mirrors in our section of Erda."

Seeing my puzzled look, Beru added, "He can see through them."

"He?"

"The Evil One. Abbadon. He who wants to destroy our Kingdom while killing everyone who doesn't agree with him, or look like him. Or what he used to look like. He appears different now. Or so I've been told. Seeing him is usually a death sentence. Only a few have managed to escape. Even then, they rarely live for long after that."

Beru kept on walking as if what she said wasn't terrifying. I rushed to catch up wanting answers to all the questions in my head. However, one look at her face and I knew she would be giving me nothing. She would be answering questions only when she was ready to, and not a moment before then.

I chose a safer subject and asked her what we were having for breakfast. Would we be eating in the atrium?

Apparently, this was not a safer subject because Beru snapped at me that I wouldn't be eating until after the first class and that the atrium food was not something I should expect every day.

When I opened my mouth to say something, she interrupted me with a raise of her hand and said, "There will be water."

By then I realized that I had no idea where we were. We had not gone back to the atrium to find the door that Earl had told me to go through for the training.

Instead, Beru had twisted and turned through hallways that all looked the same to me. Without her, I would be lost, maybe forever.

Finally, Beru opened the door to what looked just like a yoga studio back home. I sighed in relief. Yoga, stretches, meditation. It all felt comfortable. I could do this.

Beru started to laugh. It was a lovely laugh. All tinkly and stuff. But I knew she was laughing at me. I began to give her a snarky response until I saw something out of the corner of my eye. What I knew must be the instructor floated in. Literally.

Still laughing, Beru backed out the door. But right before she closed the door, I saw her exchange looks with Miss Floaty. They were enjoying themselves at my expense. Right.

This was not going to be pretty.

****

Miss Floaty's feet touched the floor as she walked over to me to shake my hand. The regular way. No sliding, wiggle fingers for her. Other than levitating across the floor, she looked as I expected her to look. Yoga clothes, sleek, strong, and more beautiful than anyone had a right to be. But I wasn't planning to hold that against her.

I had too many other things to worry about. Like this class. I had been taking dance lessons in the Earth dimension, so I harbored a hope that this class wouldn't be too hard for me. Except for the levitation part. But I didn't think that it would be part of these lessons.

After shaking my hand and telling me her name was Aki she disabused me of that notion. Yes, I was going to learn to levitate. She said the word in a sarcastic voice which I took to mean that I had the wrong word for what she had done. However, she assured me, we would not be doing that today. She promised me that today would be an easy first training class, a warm-up.

An hour later I staggered out of the room to find Beru

waiting for me. "Today you get to have food before you go to your next class. You'll need it."

Too tired to answer I followed Beru as she led me through another maze of hallways to a small room with a platter of food on it. She sat with me as I ate, but didn't say anything and I didn't care. All I could think about was trying to fuel myself.

"Luckily your next class is about magic," Beru said. "Otherwise, I am pretty sure none of that food that you are stuffing in there would be staying down."

The rest of the day was a blur. Beru was right. Food did not stay down. After the magic class where I didn't understand a word of what the instructor said, everything else was a blur of physical torture.

I didn't even think about complaining when the door locked on me again that night. Who cared? Not me. I didn't care about anything. I fell into the bed even more tired than I was the night before, and I dreamed.

Eleven

A blue haze hung around me. It looked like the haze I had seen surround the Castle. I thought it was fog, even though I had never seen blue fog.

Now that I was alone with the haze, I had time to study it. It was not like any fog I had ever experienced. It didn't move like fog or spread out like fog. It made shapes of itself.

Once I realized that it wasn't fog, it was as if it didn't have to pretend anymore. It shaped itself around me leaving me feeling like a hole in a donut. Then it split into big bubbles that danced in circles. One landed on my head, and if it had been a person, I would have said that it laughed.

I laughed, too. Who wouldn't with a dancing blue bubble on their head.

When my teeth started chattering, I realized that I was cold. Before falling into bed, I had stripped off the leggings and top I had acquired as I stepped through the portal hoping somehow I would get new clean clothes in the morning. I had found a large white shirt lying on my bed, so I had put it on. But that left my legs bare, and I was feeling colder and colder.

I stopped laughing, and the blue haze pulled back. It looked just like water pulling back before a tidal wave. I screamed, thinking it was preparing to rush me, drown me inside of it. Maybe sweep me away. I wanted to run, but my feet wouldn't move. I looked down and saw that my feet weren't feet anymore, they were oval gray rocks.

The haze rushed forward encasing me from neck to toe in a thick mist. If the rest of me had turned to stone, I couldn't see. But I was shivering and able to wrap my arms around myself which I figured I couldn't do if I had turned to stone.

Within seconds I started to warm up, and I realized that the haze wasn't cold. It was cold outside of it.

"Where am I?" I asked the haze. There was no answer.

A flock of birds flew overhead. It reminded me of geese, the way they fly in a V formation. But they didn't sound like geese. One bird left the flock and headed straight towards me like a bullet. As it flew closer, I could see that it wasn't a goose. It was shaped more like a falcon. It dived straight at me. I screamed again, but instead of attacking me it hovered in front of my face, grabbed the edge of the haze with its claws, and threw it at the flock overhead.

Immediately the bird in front of me and the flock disappeared, and I was sitting cross-legged in front of a fire. A shadow handed me a stone cup filled with blue haze, and said, "Drink this." The shadow's voice was so kind and gentle I obeyed.

I felt a warm cloud of mist move down my throat, and a deep heaviness came over me. I fell to the floor beside the fire.

The gentle hands of the shadow covered me with a blanket, and as my consciousness seeped away, I heard, "Now sleep. It will be easier tomorrow."

****

When Beru came to get me, I was already awake and thinking about my dream. Was it my brain trying to work things out or was it real? Either way, I hoped the shadow was right about the day being easier because every muscle in my body hurt. My legs felt as if they had been beaten with a stick, which was true. They had been.

Excuse me, not a stick, a staff. Not the kind that wizards carry. The type used as weapons, although maybe wizard's staffs are weapons too. I haven't met a wizard, so I'm not sure.

My instructor yesterday looked like a gazelle on steroids. A huge graceful being who looked as if he could squash me with his hand. No need for a weapon. He was the weapon. I gasped and fell back against the wall when I saw him.

Beru had led me to the training area and then moved away as fast as she could. I had wondered why until I saw Gazelle man standing there.

At first, I thought he was a statue because he was so still, and his dark skin glowed as if he was carved out of marble. Didn't take me long to discover that he wasn't a statue because he threw a staff at me. Luckily, or maybe on purpose, it missed because I flinched as it came at me. It clattered to the floor. I stared at it. What was I supposed to do with it?

He yelled at me to pick it up and then started running at me holding his staff by his side. I ran. Apparently not the proper response, although I still think it was the right thing to do. If you can run, run. "Not so," Gazelle man told me after catching me and whacking me with his staff. "Today we are going to learn how to stand and fight."

At least I thought that was what he said because he spoke so softly it was hard to understand his words. He preferred to show me the fighting movements he wanted me to learn.

Maybe because his moves were so far superior to his vocal

communications, Gazelle man chose to teach by example. He'd demonstrate the proper stance, then point at me to do the same, poking me with his staff to move my foot, or hip, or back. He'd attack, and I'd cringe or run.

He'd grunt, point, and show me what I should have done. By the end of the session yesterday, I had mastered one simple block and one way to hit someone with the staff if he was as slow as a turtle and blind as a bat during the day.

I prayed that I wouldn't be facing Gazelle man today.

"Do you even know his name, or his history, or his race? Do you know anything about him at all, Hannah," Beru asked me, once again proving that I was not good at shutting her out of my thinking.

"No, don't answer me. You don't know anything about him or any of your other instructors. They are all here for you. To teach you what you need to know. Perhaps you could show them some respect and find out something about them."

I knew what Beru was doing. She was trying to make me angry enough to survive the day. She was volunteering to be the provoker.

It was hard to see her that way with her sweet face and all that. But I knew she was much more than she appeared to be. Plus, she was right. I didn't know anything about anyone. I didn't even know where I was in time or space. I was in the realm of Erda in a castle on top of a mountain. That was all I knew. Oh, and they expected me to save their world somehow. From what? From whom?

It was time for me to get some answers, and stop being such a wimp.

Twelve

When I walked into my session with Aki, I thought that the shadow from my dream might have been telling me the truth. There was a small table set in the middle of the room, along with a teapot and two teacups.

Aki glided into the room a few inches off the floor and gestured to a cushion set by the table. I had been too stunned and tired the day before to notice my surroundings. Today I saw that the walls were lit the same as the halls, with an invisible light source. The floor was a polished wood of some kind, and there were scrolls hung around the room. They reminded me of some of the Japanese paintings I had seen in one of my school books. Did they mean something?

"Today, Hannah, I am going to tell you a part of a story. You can decide if it is a fairy tale, or reality, or maybe a mix of both, as most stories are, you know. Since all stories can be changed or re-written, it will be up to you to decide what you want to do about it. That is, if you take it as real. Or find the meaning behind it."

Aki poured tea in both our cups and took a sip from hers. "Drink please; it will help you listen without falling asleep."

I did what she asked me to do, keeping my eyes locked onto

her face instead of avoiding it as I had done yesterday. As I stared at her, I realized that there was something off about her. Her face was beautiful, but what made the beauty even more striking were her eyes. This was another example of my not paying attention since I arrived on Erda, because her eyes were hard to miss.

As Aki put her teacup down and turned her full attention to me, she slowly closed her eyes, and when she opened them again, they were the palest blue I had ever seen. Very freaky. Then, as she told the story the color of her eyes would grow brighter, or darker, and then fade again. I began to wonder if what she looked like wasn't her true form. And if that was the case, what did she really look like?

"Do you want the story Hannah, or are you too busy trying to figure things out?"

I put my teacup down, folded my legs beneath me, and turned my full attention to Aki. I knew the story was the beginning of understanding. It was what Beru had said to me. It was time to learn who these people were and why they were here. I hoped the story would help me figure it out.

****

"Shall we start with Once Upon A Time? It is how all good stories that may or may not be true begin, isn't it?" Aki asked.

I nodded and she began.

"Once upon a time, a long, long, long time ago, a giant silver serpent twisted and turned its way through the stars. Inside that metal serpent traveled two brothers who had been alive for more years than anyone could count and they were bored. So bored. They thought they knew everything there was to know. There were no more adventures that they hadn't already done, and there was nothing new to see.

"The snake had taken them everywhere they wanted to go. The beings inside the metal serpent had seen worlds that had just been born, and worlds that had destroyed themselves time and again. Watching had been fun for a few million years, but the joy of it had faded.

"They knew that self-destruction was one way to keep from being bored. But self-destruction didn't appeal to them anymore, either. They had regrown their own civilization too many times to count. Even self-destruction had turned boring.

"One night while lounging on the observation deck, so bored they could barely lift their drinks to their mouths, the two brothers came up with an idea to amuse themselves. Why not make a world of their own and experiment with it? See what happens when they mess with it?

"Of course, this was illegal. Even in a civilization as jaded as theirs, there were rules, and this was one. Everyone knew that the law was to let civilizations alone and let them evolve on their own. Destroy themselves—or not. Voyeurism was perfectly fine, and for millenniums this is what they had been doing. But, as I said, they were bored.

"These two brothers decided that they didn't care anymore. So what if they were caught? At least being punished wouldn't be boring.

"Over the next few years, these brothers hatched their plan. They decided that just one world wasn't enough. What about two? When finding two identical planets proved difficult, they came up with another idea. What about one planet and two dimensions? That was the perfect scenario. They could compete and decide once and for all which brother was the best brother.

"By using dimensions instead of different planets, the playing field would be almost equal. It also made it easier for them to check on their experiment. It meant that there would only be one world to visit on the trips through the universes. They just had to return to one planet and then slip between the two dimensions to see how their experiment was going.

"It took a few more passes through the galaxies to pick the perfect planet. It was a beautiful place. It had everything: oceans, air, lakes, trees, and mountains. It reminded them both of a world that had been destroyed many thousands of years in the past when its star exploded. There were rumors that the explosion had been deliberate, but no one could prove it. The brothers laughed together over the idea that perhaps someone else had been as bored as they were.

"While they traveled to find the planet, they made up the rules that would govern the people. But first, they needed people. Neither of them wanted to live there. They valued being observers, not participants. To solve their problem, they found volunteers in the prisoners on board. It was a simple choice. Either die or populate a planet. Well, you know what the prisoners chose.

"The brothers made the experiment as equal as possible. They didn't want to give either dimension an unfair advantage.

"They only did a few things differently. They wanted to see if that made a difference. The answer, Hannah, is that those few things turned out to be the pivot points that changed everything."

Thirteen

Aki rose, stretched, and said, "That's your lesson for today, Hannah. Stretch your mind, instead of your body."

"You aren't going to tell me what the differences were?" I huffed. How could she take me that far, and then not tell me? What if the story was true? Didn't I need to know?

"Not today. You spend time thinking about what those differences might be."

This time, instead of gliding out of the room, Aki vanished. One moment she was there. The next she wasn't. What was up with that? People kept disappearing. How did they do it?

Ziffer, I mumbled to myself. How was I supposed to figure how people vanished along with everything else that was going on. The story was making me feel itchy. What if it was true? Were Earth and Erda the two dimensions she was talking about?

"No time to ponder that now," Beru said. She was casually leaning against the door, her eyes dancing with delight.

"Do you know the story?" I asked her.

"Of course," Beru answered, "but I'm not the one who is going to give you the answer. Besides, it's time for your next class. Let's see if you can find your way this time. You lead, I'll follow."

I gave Beru the best evil eye look I could muster, but it only made her laugh.

"Come on, Hannah, feel the walls and doors. They'll lead the way."

Looking at my pouting face, she added, "Seriously, Hannah. You have to be able to do this. You are not going to be very effective if you can't find your way around."

"You mean, feel my way around, don't you?" I said through clenched teeth.

"Exactly. I'll wait."

Of course, she would wait. Even though I had only known Beru for a few days, I knew she could outlast me in any waiting game. Besides, putting aside my frustration, I knew she was trying to teach me something important. So I reached out and asked to be guided.

I shut my eyes until Beru said, "Keep your eyes open. Do you think the enemy is going to wait while you stand there with your eyes shut? Do this with your eyes open. Trust the guidance. Your world calls it the force, doesn't it? Follow that. Pretend that it's there right in front of you. Imagine how it would feel to be guided. Go, go, go."

There was that go, go, go command, again. What is it with this world where everyone is always saying that to me? But I obeyed. I opened my eyes and trusted. And I knew. I didn't know where I was going, but I knew what step to take next.

I was cautious at first, but soon I was walking at a reasonable pace. A few minutes later, I ended up exactly where I meant to go, the magic room, where Professor Pinhead was waiting for me.

No that's not his real name, I made that up. Sounded good to me yesterday, but today something was different inside of me. Today I would listen and hear his real name. Today I would be respectful and learn something.

Beru reached out and touched the back of my hand. I looked down, and she gave me the sweetest smile. It was the best reward for good thinking I had ever felt. I smiled back and stepped into the room.

The professor was there, sitting at his desk, but so was someone else. For a moment, I thought it was Johnny. I hoped it was Johnny, and my heart did a little flip-flop. But when he turned, I saw that it wasn't Johnny after all.

No one said anything. We stared at each other until the stranger walked over to me where I was standing like an idiot in the doorway.

Still dumbstruck I continued to stare at him until he said, "Hi, I'm Zeid. I know you're Hannah. Happy to meet you!"

Still an idiot, I mumbled, "Oh wow, you know who I am. Who are you anyway?"

"Hannah!" Beru hissed.

"Sorry, that was rude. It's just I haven't seen anyone my age here yet. Or sort of my age. Are you my age? Oh, sorry again, so rude again."

Zeid just laughed and grabbed me by the elbow leading me to my desk. "You know if I had just traveled to a new dimension a few days ago and everything was different, I am sure I would be as confused and frustrated as you. More, I bet.

"I live here. Never dimension traveled, although I think that might be fun. Not going to happen though. They closed the portal after you came through."

If there was a mirror in the room, I was sure it would have shown that I turned white. "They closed the portal," I gasped.

"Oh ziffer, I'm sorry. Of course, this is upsetting. Were you expecting more people to come with you?"

I nodded yes, and whispered, "And I thought that I could go

home again, someday."

Zeid put a reassuring hand on my shoulder. "It's possible, Hannah. Don't give up hope. In the meantime, I'll be here training with you."

Both Zeid's words and his hand on my shoulder burned.

Professor—didn't know his name yet—humphed, and said, "Open your books, Zeid and Hannah. There is much to be done. We'll travel to the Riff soon. You need to be ready."

Riff? What had I missed? What was a Riff? What did I have to be ready for?

I looked at Zeid for reassurance. He winked one of his amazing azure eyes at me, and I blushed.

Which was going to be worse? The Riff or what was happening to me. Honestly, all I could think of at that moment is that I wanted my mom. I wanted to be twelve years old again, snuggling in bed as we told each other about our day. I wanted to go back to sewing secret ladybug appliqués into each others' clothes.

I felt a tap on my leg and looked down. Beru was there by my foot. She turned back the seam on the bottom of my leggings and revealed a ladybug appliqué.

Beru had given me my mom. I would be okay for a little bit longer.

Fourteen

Zeid trained with me after that. He was my sparring partner in Gazelle Man's class where he whipped my butt, too. He didn't hurt as much when he whacked me as the gazelle did, but he was just as relentless. Yes, he was pretty dang cute, but he proved to me right away that he wasn't planning to give me any slack just because I hoped we would be friends.

I did learn people's names, though. I took to heart Beru's comment about not caring about the people that helped me. Professor Pinhead was really Professor Link. At least I got the professor part right.

Gazelle Man was Niko. And of course, I already knew Aki's name. Since many of the people I met during our training sessions came and went depending on what we were learning, I didn't get most of their names.

We spent most of the time in Link's class learning about how to do various forms of magic. Zeid didn't need to learn. He knew how. He was increasing his skills, while I was trying to access mine. He loved showing me what Professor Link meant by "be somewhere else." Zeid was excellent at that, and he could come and go at will. I didn't get it at all. No matter how hard I tried, I never went anywhere.

Zeid told me that I was thinking of it as something I had to do, like what I did in the Earth Realm when I did what they call astral projection. In Erda, it didn't work that way. They allowed magic to work through them.

The whole idea of what they called magic eluded me. What was magic? Was it what we called in the Earth Realm paranormal powers? I could do those in the Earth Realm, but it seemed as if I was without those skills in Erda.

The professor kept telling me that everyone could do what was called magic. It was an innate skill that everyone on Erda knew about which in a way made it not magic. It was like breathing. It was part of life. Link said that if you think about it that way, everything is magic.

In Erda, some people practice using magic and get better at it the same way people practice music while others don't care to learn more than basic humming skills.

When I asked him if magic was innate for everyone in the Earth Realm too, he looked away for a moment. When he looked back, his green eyes squinted at me, and a lock of dark hair fell across his forehead as he answered. "Yes. But," and then turned away.

That was it? "Yes, but what?" I asked, trying to be polite. I squinted my eyes at him as he had at me. Made no difference. He refused to tell me more.

At the end of the day, the professor called me to his desk where he sat perched on the edge. "Hannah, this is as hard for me as it is for you. If I tell you everything, if anyone of us tells you everything, you might not discover it for yourself. We can only guide you to where you might find the answers.

"I can tell you that you, Hannah, that you have the same skills you had before you came here, except on Erda they are much more powerful and expansive. But here you have to find the source of them and bring it into yourself. No one can do that for you. But it's there, waiting for you.

"There's a reason you were asked to come here. We need your skill more than we ever have before."

What he said didn't make any sense. "You asked me to come here? I thought I begged and begged. And if I have those powers, why do I feel so powerless? So ordinary?"

For the first time, Professor Link smiled. "You did beg, Hannah. You begged, and we asked. The two had to come together. As for not being able to access your powers, it's because on Earth you didn't know where those powers came from.

"You thought nothing about how you acquired them. And if you are honest with yourself, you thought you were slightly better than everyone else because of it.

"Here, everyone knows where magic comes from. They understand the source. Those of us who want to protect that source honor it. We know it does not come from us. It does not make us superior because we practice it more. In fact, it becomes an obligation to protect those who need protecting."

"So, let me get this straight. You want me to stop feeling superior? Check, done. I have never felt so inferior in my life. You want me to learn where magic comes from, and then protect it? That means someone wants to destroy it?"

Link's face grew dark as he continued to stare at me with those squinted green eyes. I wondered if the squint was because he couldn't see well, or he was protecting himself, not allowing me to see something about him.

"You still feel superior, Hannah and that will get in the way of returning to who you are, and that's dangerous. Because, yes, a very powerful someone wants to destroy magic for everyone but himself."

Link reached into a drawer in his desk and took out a small

wooden box and handed it to me. "This was left here for you."

Astonished, I took the box from him. It was beautiful. Carved on the lid was a large spreading tree. Bare of leaves, the intricacy of its branches could be seen reaching across the lid. Its root system spread out across the side and wrapped around the entire box. I ran my finger across the carving and realized the box had been carved around the tree. How could that be?

Opening the box, I found a bracelet embedded with a picture-jasper stone. The veins running through the stone looked like the tree on the box.

Link took the bracelet out and placed it on my left wrist next to my friendship bracelet from Johnny. It immediately molded itself to my arm.

I had so many questions. Who left this for me? Why did it feel so familiar? When I looked up to ask, Professor Link was already scooping up his books and papers. He left without saying another word, leaving me still feeling lost but not quite as alone as before.

"So, Link thought you were ready for it," Suzanne said.

I whirled around and found her standing at the door smiling at me. She could have been there all along, or maybe she appeared using the same magic she used when she'd vanish.

"Come along, Hannah. We're going into the village for dinner. You'll be leaving the castle soon, I want you to meet some of the people going with you."

"Where are we going?"

"To the Riff. It's as dangerous to get there as it is to participate. We'll need more protection."

Protection. My stomach cramped at the thought. It wasn't as if I hadn't known there was danger. I now knew what that shrieking sound had been in the woods. Besides, I had been isolated in the Castle for weeks. I was pretty sure that had to do with keeping me safe while I trained.

I hoped my training was enough. I guessed it would have to be.

I needed more answers, and I thought that our trip to the village would get me some. The bracelet on my wrist was reassuring. I knew that jasper stones represented healing, courage, and wisdom. They are grounded to the energy of the earth. I knew that although I was in a different dimension I was still on the planet earth, and I hoped that the stone would help me find the strength I needed for the mission that was before me.

Fifteen

A few days before we left to visit the village of Dalry, we were outside sitting in the grove of trees that grew almost to the Castle wall, when my life in Erda turned upside down.

Professor Link often took us outside to teach. Sometimes we strolled through the garden where he would point out various plants and insects. I thought it was because he hated being cooped up inside a building, no matter how beautiful, as much as I did. That probably was true, but he was trying to show me something so obvious I missed it. Until one day it clicked.

He was showing me a connection. How that bird planted trees or that bug made the soil more fertile, or how that group of flowers provided homes and food for everything from insects to people. But he always brought it back to the trees. Time and again the story wove back to how the planet lived because trees provided everything it needed,

Eventually, dense as I can sometimes be, I realized he was teaching me all about the trees. Everything he showed us, everything I took for granted, happened because the trees had provided for it.

In Erda, trees were everywhere. I thought it probably looked like the eastern part of the United States in the Earth Realm before man started cutting down trees.

Erda was a land of forests. I suppose that like most people, buried within my thinking was the awareness that trees provide life. But in Earth, not everyone acknowledged that fact and instead many people did their best to eliminate trees and nature as much as possible. I don't think they dislike nature as much as they love making money from her resources.

Maybe that was the difference Aki mentioned in the story about the two dimensions. Perhaps the people of Erda never lost their connection to nature and trees which supplied everything needed for the planet to thrive, and the people of the Earth Realm lost theirs, or it was never accepted in the same way as they did in Erda. I thought there was probably more than that, but I was sure that I was on the right track.

On the day I learned about Shatterskin, the sun was warm as it wound its way through the tree canopy and pooled at our feet, melting away some of my homesickness. Overhead I heard birds singing. Many of them the same as the ones I knew, and a few I had never seen before. I could hear Lady drumming away further in the forest, but I knew if I called her she would be at my side in an instant.

Zeid and I were sitting on a stone bench in the center of the grove while Beru and Ruta were standing at the tree line. I knew something was up. The tension in the air was heavy and oppressive.

As Professor Link said the word "Shatterskin" that tension erupted all around me. It was as if the word itself had shattered the peace in the grove. Everything, including the bench, moved into a state of readiness.

"What the ziffer," I said. "What happened? What's a Shatterskin?"

Zeid turned to me and whispered, "Best not to keep saying

that word. We avoid it as much as possible."

"That's true," Link said. "It likes to hear its name, so now that you have heard it let's not mention the name again in this lesson. It also has an army of minions we call the Shrieks."

"Shrieks? Like the ones I heard while we were coming here?"

When Link nodded, I felt sick inside. The sound had been so loud I could barely think, and everyone had run faster than I thought possible. They were afraid of him, or it, or them. These people, capable of magic of all kinds, were terrified of a sound.

****

Link and Zeid left me hanging after that. I think all my teachers like to fill me up with worry and fear and see how I deal with it, because they did it all the time. They gave me bits of pieces of knowledge and then left me with it to let my imagination run wild.

The rest of that day I kept thinking about the shrieking we had heard, and how everyone had felt the fear. Everyone ran from it, not just me. I tried filling in what I knew with what it could be, but nothing came to me. All I managed to conjure up was more terror that I was going to re-encounter it.

I asked myself if I could face it. Could I confront an unknown entity that wanted to hurt my friends and me, and not run away? Could I stand and fight? Of course, that was what Niko, Link, and Aki were training me to do.

I was not the same girl that came to Erda weeks before. The body I acquired in Erda had started to become familiar, and it was hard to remember the little girl I had been in the Earth dimension.

I was still afraid, but no longer fearful, which I was hoping was a distinction that would work in my favor.

The day Link told me about Shatterskin, Aki's class was the last one of the day, and I knew it was going to be different again. The teapot and teacups were on the table. Aki was already seated and waiting for me.

"Are you ready to hear more of the story, Hannah?"

"More of the story? Meaning still not the whole story?" I asked.

Aki inclined her head and closed her eyes, a movement I had seen her make before but could never duplicate myself. When she opened them her eyes were no longer pale blue, but almost black.

"Part of. For a reason. Sit."

I sat. Aki poured tea, took a sip, and waited for me to take a sip. More aware than I had been in our first storytelling session, I felt the tea flow through me, opening spaces as it traveled. Aki waited, and when she knew I was ready, she began again, "Once upon a time..."

Sixteen

Susan continued, "As the two brothers traveled through the galaxies in the silver serpent, they decided on the planet we call Earth. Its real name is Gaia. It was perfect for their purpose. To make their experiment work, they had to agree on some rules. They decided on two parallel dimensions. Up until that time, Gaia's dimensions had developed almost exactly alike. Nature was in charge, and she knew the exact thing to do to bring each dimension into a state of optimum health.

"There were no creatures on the planet Gaia that weren't born of nature's careful planning. Each entity had its place. They knew what their purpose was and joyfully lived it. Harmony reined. Yes, there were storms and earthquakes. Icebergs slid across continents destroying ecosystems while building other ones. Some of the creatures yielded their life form to build up the riches of the world. Every aspect of both dimensions was in perfect balance.

"What we call death was not seen that way to the creatures of the Gaia. Although none of nature spoke of energy in words that we might use today, even the tiniest microorganism knew it was a part of the One power or force that was the life of the planet. If one creature gave their life force to another, it didn't matter. They knew that they would rise again, in a different form perhaps, but they understood that life continues.

"They freely gave and freely received. It was heaven as we might think of it today. Harmony was all that they knew.

"Then one day the brothers arrived, and everything changed—because that was what the brothers wanted to do. Make change. Make chaos, and see what happened. They were playing a game called "be gods of a world." They would play until one of the gods won. They didn't care if it took thousands of years to play out. That would only be a drop in the bucket of their lifetimes.

"In each dimension, Earth and Erda, they placed life forms that had not developed as part of the natural system. They put these different life forms in equal numbers in each dimension. They gave them the same training, and the same supplies, and started their experiment.

"It wasn't just humans as you know them, Hannah. There were cultures culled from planets they had visited in their thousands of years of travel through countless solar systems.

"Of course some were more suited to Gaia's system than others, but for the most part they managed to survive. In each dimension, they evolved to match their surroundings.

"But because of the differences that the brothers put into place, they evolved differently."

Aki paused and took a deep breath. So deep I could almost see it travel through her body as she allowed the muscles that had begun to tense up to relax. I could almost feel what was coming next. Erda and Earth were different in many ways. But why were they and how did that happen?

I forced myself to wait as she kept her eyes closed and breathed. When she started again, I could barely hear her. "They made rules. Rules of the game they wanted to play. Since none of the life forms they had brought to the planet had evolved out from the nature found on Gaia, one of the first rules was obvious. Survive.

"But in Erda, the rule was to survive in harmony with the life forms already present. Learn how to become part of that system. Thrive with the planet. Evolve to fit with it.

"In the Earth dimension, they didn't impose that rule. The knowledge of the harmony of nature existed, but they didn't instill it into the new inhabitants. It had to be learned. And the creatures had a choice. They could thrive with it or without it.

"Perhaps the brothers wanted to see if the beings they left in the two dimensions on the planet Gaia would learn harmony with nature because it seemed evident that evolving with it and protecting it was the only way to thrive long term. For whatever reason, they left it up to the free will of the people in the Earth dimension and made it part of the way of life in the Erda dimension.

"There were many ramifications that were born from this one difference. Most of them you know, or will see for yourself, Hannah. However, the one that you are dealing with now is what the Earth dimension calls magic. In Earth, very few people accept magic as real. In Erda, everyone knows magic. Beyond that, and much more importantly, they understand where magic comes from. They know it's real. They live with it daily. Every citizen of Erda uses magic to provide everything that they need.

"Some have more access than others because they want to have it. They become artists of magic. They practice. Just as someone might practice their innate skills in art, or sports, or music, or teaching, or farming and become masters of that art, there are creatures here that practice magic.

Aki stopped and let me sit, steeped in silence. The implications of what she was telling me answered so many questions. However, I had more.

"Go ahead, Hannah, ask that question that is burning to be spoken."

"There must have been something else they did. Otherwise, why are there terrible things that people do in Earth? And not just in the Earth dimension either. Here in Erda, you are all afraid of the Shrieks. What else did the brothers do?"

"You're right, Hannah. They did something else. They put duplicates of themselves in other dimensions. They wanted to know which brother would win, not just in the galactic game that they were playing, but within each dimension.

"One brother was given the desire to control and have all power. The other brother was instilled with the desire to build community and harmony with shared responsibility for the welfare of each other.

"The brothers were careful not to put their duplicates too close together in Erda, because in the Earth Realm the battle was settled almost instantly. They didn't want a repeat of that in Erda."

"It's the Cain and Abel story isn't it?"

Aki looked at me, her eyes slit so I could barely see them. "It is. They learned from it. In Erda, the Cain and Abel characters were placed far enough apart that Abel's offspring were not aware of what Cain was doing until only a few centuries ago.

"You said Abel's offspring. How could the original Cain and Abel still be alive?"

"Because in Erda, life continues for thousands of years. It's still the original brothers. And the brother who is Cain in the Erda story has no desire to share his power with anyone, even his own offspring. So he never married and never had children.

"Instead, he builds creatures that serve him and his desire to rule the entire planet. He will do anything to win the game.

Cain destroys. Of course, his name is not Cain. In Erda, his name is Abbadon, the destroyer."

"And the creatures he built are the Shrieks?"

A single tear dropped down Aki's perfect cheek. "The Shrieks serve the monster Abbadon built called Shatterskin. He and the Shrieks are the first ones you must defeat at the Riff."

I was sure I didn't correctly hear what she said, so I sat there waiting for the rest of the story. Maybe I would wake up, and all of this would be a dream. I would be home in Earth waiting for my brother Ben to wake up so we could play together with mom and dad.

There was no way I could face monsters like Shatterskin and his shrieking minions. Besides, I still didn't know what they did other than scare the ziffer out of everyone.

"No, it's not a dream, Hannah. And no, you won't be waking up from it. Yes, there is more to this story, but that's enough for now. I can tell you that you will have the ability to do this. Besides, you will be with people that can, and will, help. You aren't alone, and you won't be alone at the Riff.

"Take another sip of tea so you can sleep tonight, and tomorrow you'll be going into the village for a meeting of your team."

I had too many questions and fears to question what Aki wanted me to do. I took another sip of tea.

It was the last thing I remembered that day.

Seventeen

It was a bit weird that we hadn't been to the village before. Dalry was so close I could see it when we trained outside the walls. We practiced outside every day no matter what kind of weather, so sometimes the town would be hidden from view by the thick fog that often surrounded the castle. Other days it would be sparkling from the sun glinting off some of the rooftops.

I yearned to visit. I had asked about the village more than once, but I had been ignored. Being ignored was the typical response for most of the things I wondered about. People would pretend they hadn't heard me, or look directly at me and then turn away. It was something I had come to expect.

However, ever since I learned that we would be going to the village, the anticipation was making me crazy. The meeting with Aki had faded into the background. I had a feeling that Aki had somehow dulled my memory so that I could function. Although a vague sense of dread remained, the excitement of seeing the village I had wanted to visit since the first time that I saw it took over. The problem was it felt as if everyone was dragging their feet. They were walking slower than the proverbial turtle. By everyone, I meant Zeid, Suzanne, Ruta, and Beru.

For the last few weeks, I had rarely seen Ruta or Suzanne. However, Beru was my daily companion, and I had grown to treasure the time with her. She looked tiny and sweet, almost like the elves I used to think I saw playing in the forest back home in Earth. However, she was as tough as steel if crossed. Although I had questioned Beru countless times about her people—who were they, where did they come from—those were questions she always ignored. Sometimes she answered, "You'll see," but mostly it was silence. After weeks of bugging her all the time, I finally shut up and accepted what she was giving to me: kindness, companionship, and guidance. She was my faithful guide around the Castle, and now she guided us to the village.

I couldn't believe we walked. I half expected to fly or be picked up by that bubble that had brought us to the castle. Or ride something. Not that I had seen anything to ride.

"First, young lady," Suzanne said. "It's not necessary to ride to the village. Second, people need to see you as someone they like. They walk. You walk. Third, you need all the exercise you can get."

At least she hadn't called me "little one." The fact that even when Earl showed up, he had stopped calling me that gave me some hope that perhaps something about me made them think I was growing up. I did feel much stronger and faster after all these weeks of training. My magic skills still sucked though. Or, as Professor Link kept pointing out, "It's not your magic skills that suck Hannah. It's your use of them."

Yeah right.

"Don't worry, Hannah. You will have lots of real-time practice soon," Beru said.

Was that supposed to encourage me? Make me feel better? I looked at Beru, and she smiled. I guess it was.

The village was further away than I thought, especially

walking as slowly as we were. It was a pretty road, lined with trees, and paved much like the roads at home that were out in the country. We had walked about a mile before the fact that it was paved finally struck me. Paved? Paved with what?

Did paved roads and castles go together? Until then I hadn't thought about it. We had power of some kind, there were indoor bathrooms, all the comforts of home, but since I hadn't seen cars or planes, I had not thought about what year it was. Was it the same year as in the Earth dimension?

"The answer is yes, Hannah," Beru said. "Although here our time is not counted the same way, and our technology is more hidden than yours. And no, we decided not to use trains, cars, or planes. We have other means of transportation.

"People on Earth would think of them as magic, we think of them as nature-friendly."

I was ready to ask more questions, but we had just crested a small hill, and the village lay before us. It looked like my picture of a quiet English village untouched by time. It was my picture only because I have never actually been to England let alone seen a quiet English village.

Suzanne led us to a building that looked like a cross between houses I knew and a hobbit house. A wooden sign that said "The Tavern" hung above the door, squeaking in the wind. There was no one on the streets. I had a suspicion it was because of us. Were they afraid or respectful, I wondered?

"Both," Beru answered and pushed open the door. It was not at all what I was expecting. I thought we would be entering a dark little space, but instead, the door opened into a spacious and well-lit room with booths around the outside and tables in the middle. Once again, I had no idea how there could be light everywhere. There weren't lamps or light switches. It was like the Castle. Was it electricity? How were they doing that?

Everyone looked up as we entered, and all the happy chattering stopped. In the silence, Suzanne led us to one of the larger round tables set for nine. Being stared at is not my favorite thing, but at least no one bowed. And if they had weapons, they were well hidden.

Suzanne waved us towards the table and directed us each to a seat. There were two empty seats beside Suzanne and me. The door opened again, and Aki and Niko walked in.

We all stood as they walked to the table and I whispered to Beru, "How come they didn't walk with us?"

She nodded at the door and said, "They chose to come with them."

Standing in the doorway were two beings. I whispered to Beru, "Are those dwarfs without beards?"

Beru pinched my leg so hard tears came to my eyes as she said, "For zounds sake don't ever, ever, ever call them that." She paused and smiled as the two came towards our table. "They are the Ginete, and it took us years to get them to join us."

Everyone at the table and in the tavern rose in unison and bowed their heads as the two people with little bodies, big heads, and eyes that took up a large part of their face moved to our table. I felt a silent collective sigh of relief that followed in their wake. Was it because they were afraid of the Ginete or grateful for them?

Once again, Beru answered, "Both, Hannah."

Eighteen

"We have heard of your return," one of the Ginete said, turning its huge golden eyes my way. The other one swiveled its head towards me too. It felt as if two lighthouses had turned their beams on me.

I looked around. Were they looking at me?

The Ginete turned to Suzanne. "She does not yet remember? Ah. I see. You want us to conduct a remembering ceremony?"

"We do," Suzanne answered.

If Beru had not given me one of her evil eye looks, I would have spoken up in protest or fled the room. Not sure which one would have come first. But there was nowhere to go, and I knew I had no say in the matter. I was sure they had the wrong person. I had nothing to remember, at least nothing important enough to have a ceremony.

"There is a full moon tomorrow. Can you do it then?" Suzanne asked.

The two Ginete looked at each other and turned back to Suzanne. They answered in unison, "We can."

"Great," Zeid said, "Let's eat!"

I was furious. They were all in on it. Every one of them, including Zeid. Why didn't someone tell me?

Zeid leaned across the table in my direction and said, "It will be epic, Hannah."

I whispered back, "Is that supposed to comfort me?"

Everyone at the table laughed, and I wanted the floor to open up and swallow me. It felt as if everyone in the restaurant knew what our table was laughing about and joined in. Really and truly, I was screwed.

****

Everyone acted as if the world wasn't over and started chatting with each other. A basket of bread appeared on the table and was passed around along with a bowl of butter. Seriously? This is what they did after scaring me to death. Eat? Apparently so.

No one had ordered anything, but within minutes Zeid said, "Ah, our food."

Instead of metal toadstools serving us the way they did at the Castle, each person at the table took turns getting up and getting the next course that had been laid out on a ledge in the back of the room.

I could see hands putting it there but nothing else. I could only assume there were cooks back there somewhere preparing the food.

In any case, a bell would ring, and someone at the table would get the food and serve each person. Even though none of us had placed an order, somehow each plate put in front of us was perfect, although none of them were the same. But I was in such a daze I barely noticed what everyone was eating. I nibbled at my food and tried to listen to the conversations.

They didn't sound that much different from conversations I had heard at restaurants back home in Earth. Talking between friends, renewing bonds. Words were weaving in and around, making a kind of music as each one joined in, bringing their unique voice. Of course, I was hoping to hear more about the Remembering Ceremony that the Ginete said they would hold. But nothing more was mentioned.

Aki had taken a seat on one side of me, and Niko sat on the other side. The bell rang, and Aki got up to serve. It suddenly occurred to me that I might be supposed to serve next.

Inside my head, I heard Beru's voice say, "Yes, you are next. I'll tell you what to do."

I was so happy to hear her I almost burst into tears. I used to be able to hear people talking to me in my head but had lost that ability when we arrived in Erda. People heard me, but I didn't hear them. Now, for the first time, I heard someone. I prayed that meant some of my skills were returning to me. It was even more wonderful because it was Beru who was guiding me as she had been since I first met her.

Across the table, Beru smiled that smile that lit up everything around her and then wiggled her slim fingers on the table. It had become our secret sign of solidarity and never had it meant more to me than at that moment.

The bell rang, and I got up as if I knew what I was doing. I did because Beru walked me through it all.

She told me what plates to put in front of what person, serving myself last. Relief flooded through me. Whatever the Remembering Ceremony was going to be, I knew Beru would be with me.

Then the most amazing thing happened. I heard everyone's voice.

Suzanne, Aki, Niko, Zeid, Beru, and even Ruta said, "Hannah, we will be with you. We are your team." The two voices that chimed in next sent a shiver of both anticipation and joy through me. The two Ginete said in unison. "We too travel with you."

I smiled at everyone at the table and silently answered them. "Thank you from the bottom of my heart."

Suddenly I was hungry. Everyone laughed and dug into their food, including me. Whatever was going to happen tomorrow night was not happening at that moment. I realized that it might be the last time I had a chance to sit at a table and eat a proper meal.

That night as I lay in my bed, I heard a voice I hadn't heard for many months. It was a voice that I loved and trusted with all of my being while living in the Earth dimension. But Sarah's husband Leif had stopped coming back to Earth to visit long before I traveled to Erda.

My expectation of seeing him in Erda had faded since I hadn't heard from him, or Sarah. I assumed I wouldn't because Sarah had not come through the portal with me. But there he was, in my head. It was as if a door opened in my mind while we were at dinner, and I could hear voices again.

Leif's voice stole over me, like the blue haze in the dreams I had weeks before. "Sleep well, little one," he said, and I realized he had been there all along. It was me that had been missing.

Perhaps the Remembering Ceremony wasn't going to be so bad after all. With that thought, I slept. I had a feeling it would be a while before I was able to sleep so soundly again.

Nineteen

Sun was streaming into my bedroom when I woke. Someone had come in and opened the curtains but had not made me get up. Every other day, Beru had shaken me awake in what felt like the middle of the night. It worried me. Was something wrong?

And then I remembered. Tonight was the ceremony. I fell back into the bed and pulled the covers over my head. Maybe it would all go away. I kept expecting someone to grab the blankets and tell me to get up and stop hiding. No one did. Which felt worse than having Beru berate me for being lazy.

When I realized that I couldn't sleep and that I was curious about what was going on without me, I dressed and headed to the atrium hoping to find someone, anyone, who would tell me what we were doing. Was I supposed to go to class? Were they expecting me?

Thinking they were probably all waiting for me, I hurried through the halls. I knew my way now. I could see the numbers on the doors but rarely had to use them. I didn't meet anyone in the halls. I tried to look in Aki's room, but the door was locked. So was the entrance to Niko's training studio.

I was getting worried. Although the Castle had very few people living in it, I always saw people strolling through the halls or sitting in the gardens, or working in what looked like offices. They never spoke to me or looked at me, but I hadn't realized what a comfort it had been to see them. Today, no one was anywhere.

When I reached the atrium, there was one place set at the table and one metal toadstool with a platter on its head filled with food that I like. Although I had never heard the metal toadstool speak, I was desperate. "Where are the others? What's going on?"

Metal guy put my food on my plate, pointed to it with its one finger and said in a metallic voice, "Eat."

With nothing else to do, I ate. A lot. I ate so much food that after a while metal man took my plate away and said, "Stop!"

I was grateful for the command. With no one to talk to, nothing to do, and no idea what was going on, I think I could have continued to stuff food in my face just to fill up the space. I dropped my forehead to the table and tried to keep myself from burping out loud. I still didn't trust that there was no one there, and I have enough pride to try and keep noises like burps to myself.

When I looked up, I was alone again. No metal toadstool, no food, nothing. Slowly it dawned on me that perhaps this was a test of some kind. Like a treasure hunt. Maybe I was supposed to figure out how to find them. Would they want me to search the castle or did they want me to do something else?

A light bulb went off in my head. None of my teachers would want me running around looking without any sense of direction. They would want me to listen. The Hannah that I was in the Earth dimension was an excellent listener. It was a skill that had enabled me to be places I needed to be and know what was going on with all my friends, often before they did.

I realized that instead of thinking of myself as two people,

Hannah there and Hannah here, I had to start being one person. I had to remember what I already knew and merge it with what I had learned since coming to Erda and training at the Castle.

Suddenly it made sense. I had been thinking that the Remembering Ceremony was something that happened at night. What if it started this way? What if I was responsible for beginning to remember on my own?

They had given me a clue at dinner the night before. I heard them speak to me telepathically, just as I had been able to do before. Perhaps my job was to put myself together again, before whatever ceremony was happening that night.

I was clear. That was what I was to do with my time. Within me, I could feel a tiny flame burning. An awareness was beginning to stir. Listening to my feelings, I realized that I was afraid. I had been fearful from the moment I had stepped through the portal. I was scared of what would be asked of me. I was worried I couldn't handle it. I was afraid of the responsibility of being myself.

Yes, I was terrified of the Shrieks and Shatterskin. But I couldn't even begin to defeat them unless I faced my fears about myself. I might as well go back to bed and pull the covers over my head. It was tempting. But I knew it was impossible. That monster would still come for me, and those beings who had told me that they were on my team and would stand by me.

They were willing to be afraid and still do what they needed to do. Whatever I was going to remember at the ceremony would make me even more afraid. Was I willing to do what needed to be done anyway?

Admittedly, I mumbled to myself, *I didn't really have a choice.* Just because I started to feel more grownup didn't make me feel any less snarky about my situation. I wanted to blame someone, but none of that was going to help me not get shattered by

Shatterskin. I had no idea what that guy did. Shatterskin what? I headed to the library. It was time to learn everything I could about those zonking shrieks and their controller.

I spun around the atrium and yelled at the top of my lungs. I knew they were out there somewhere. "Okay, you good for nothing friends of mine. I am going to be ready to remember."

Sounded stupid even as I said it, and I swear I heard them laughing. It was hard to miss Beru's laughter that sounded like bells and Ruta's that sometimes sounded like a frog choking.

As I stomped off as dignified as I could with my belly jiggling with too much food, it occurred to me that I didn't know where to find the library. I listened and heard, "Door ten." So metal toadstool hadn't gone after all. "Thanks, big guy," I said. Its laugh was as weird as Ruta's. Think of a metal lid on a trash can vibrating. That would be close.

Twenty

The library was exactly how I expected it to be. It looked like the library back home with rows of book and tables for working or reading. The only difference that I could see straight away was, once again, there was no one there. Not even a metal toadstool.

How was I supposed to find anything? The word "listen" popped into my head again. It must have been the word of the day like the old Groucho Marx show my parents told me about. "How about a new word, people?" I asked in my head.

I knew I was irritable because I was afraid, so I told myself to shut up and listen. I thought that maybe I was being punished for my rudeness because I didn't hear anything.

Then I remembered what Beru kept telling me. Feel. It was the same as listen but didn't always have words. Listen to the feeling. It wasn't as hard to do as the first time when I was trying to feel doors. My practice was paying off because within a few seconds I knew, no, I felt, what to do.

I sat down at a table and asked for information about the Shrieks and Shatterskin. A screen popped up in front of me with options. Did I want pictures or information? I chose information. After reading for a few minutes, I almost wished that I hadn't. Too graphic. So I asked for pictures. That was even worse.

But I made myself stare at them until I could look without shaking the table. Then I went back to the written information which consisted mostly of descriptions of the destruction.

I learned enough to be even more terrified than I thought was possible. The Shrieks did what their name implied. They shrieked with a decimal level that made it impossible to think. The pain was intense, and the disorientation made everyone incapable of doing anything other than curling up in a ball, holding their ears. The Shrieks cleared the way for Shatterskin.

After I read what Shatterskin could do, I thought that he probably didn't need those little bastards given what he could do by himself. Maybe he liked the company.

Although Shatterskin also used sound, he used a decimal level that shattered everything in his path. The vibrations went deep into the earth and shattered tree roots, rocks, whatever was there. Earthquakes and volcanoes often followed him.

When Shatterskin directed his sound into the air, it instantly shattered anything flying within range. Usually, only bits of feathers and tiny bones were found after his passing. That's if anyone was brave enough to follow after him. On the surface of the earth trees shattered, and all beings blew apart. He literally shattered every kind of skin that was within reach of his sound. No wonder we ran.

The writer conjectured that Shatterskin's sound range was not far since to make that sound required an enormous amount of energy. Survivors guessed that his range was not more than perhaps one-hundred feet around him. That didn't mean much considering how quickly he moved and shattered as he went. I thought that the Shrieks must make up for his lack of range, since they traveled ahead of him and laid open a space where there was no one to oppose him.

The images of the Shrieks and Shatterskin were hand drawn. They weren't photographs. The artist said some of his pictures were conjectures based on seeing these beings from miles away. Anyone close enough to see details was dead.

Abbadon had built an utterly effective means of destruction with the Shrieks and Shatterskin. Was his quest for power so great that he was willing to destroy the land and the people? Didn't he know that destroying nature would ultimately destroy him?

I looked at the pictures one more time. The Shrieks literally looked like big mouths within blobs of green goo that slithered. I couldn't see any features other than a hole that changed shapes. I had to assume that it made different kinds of shrieks depending on the size of the opening.

Shatterskin looked like my picture of an evil metal robot. A terminator made of metal. What kind of metal, I didn't know and neither did the writer. Maybe it had to be metal so the sound the Shrieks were making wouldn't shatter it? Could we make something out of the same metal to protect us?

I looked up one more thing. I figured I was so terrified that learning about the Riff would not increase my terror and I might as well get it over with.

In that, as in so many things, I was wrong.

****

I must have fallen asleep after reading all that information and scaring myself to death because I woke up with my head on the library table. Maybe it was a defense mechanism. Only so much terror allowed into one person before the brain shuts down. Memories of what I had read about the Riff started to filter back in, and I shut them down with a "no, not now" command. I thought of Niko and the defense moves he had taught me, and I used a few of them on the images in my head. That helped. They backed off, at least for a time.

The high slitted windows in the walls of the library showed me a darkening sky. Was it possible I had slept all afternoon on a library table? I was hungry enough to think that it was possible. I rose to go, thinking that my friendly metal toadstool would be waiting with some food in the atrium, when I heard one of my favorite sounds, Beru laughing.

"Zuts," Beru said, "You look a fright."

I had to restrain myself from practically leaping over my chair to hug her. But as sweet as Beru looked, hugging was only allowed if she initiated it, so I held back and wiggled my fingers at her instead.

"Where have you been? I am so happy to see you. Yes I probably do look terrible. Not used to no mirrors and then no friends to make sure that I am put together correctly," I rattled on without thinking.

Beru just stood there and smiled.

"Hungry?" she asked.

She didn't even wait for me to say anything before she was out the door and heading towards the atrium. I followed as fast as I could, but let me tell you when Beru starts moving, she moves. She was way ahead of me by the time I reached the atrium. I could smell food, and I was happy as could be. I had almost convinced myself that the idea of a ceremony and then off to defeat undefeatable monsters and a gods-forsaken Riff in the earth was never going to happen. Until I rounded the corner and saw them.

Them. Everyone. Everyone I knew and people I didn't know. People I had seen around the castle but who had never spoken to me were there. Food was piled high on the tables. The five metal guys—or were they girls too—were there serving.

I stepped into the room, and they all yelled, "Surprise." Yes, I was excited to see them all. But at the same time, I knew what it was. A last supper.

For a moment, just a teeny tiny moment, I thought about running. Where I would go didn't matter. I just needed to run. But the urge to run didn't last. These people were here for me. I would be there for them. If this was the last supper, I might as well enjoy it.

Twenty-One

Erda doesn't count the time the same way that I learned to do in the Earth dimension, so I wasn't sure what month it was back home. But the full moon looked like a harvest moon to me, so I chose to believe that it was the middle of October, which meant that I had been in Erda for over a month. It had been the fastest, the slowest, the scariest, the loneliest, and the most exciting month of my life. All of those feelings wrapped up into one package.

As Beru and I walked through the forest outside the Castle to where the ceremony was to be held, I thought through all that I had learned. The month was the fastest because as soon as Suzanne and I stepped through the portal, I was a young woman and no longer a little girl. At least my body was a young woman's body. During my time in Erda, I was trying to grow up to match it.

I had a feeling that the ceremony was going to force even more growth. I decided not to think about what I was going to remember. It was a dark rabbit hole to go down, so I tried to avoid tripping and falling into it.

Dinner was spectacular in every sense. I had never seen Ruta have a good time, but after drinking something that looked like syrup, he got very animated. He even danced on top of one of the tables. I think it was dancing. Whatever it was, it was wonderful to watch. He rarely said a word to me, but I knew he had come to like me just a little bit even though he still mumbled under his breath when I was an idiot. Not his fault. I was often an idiot. Nevertheless, I certainly had come to like him, and the dancing topped it off.

Beru held my hand as she introduced me to every person who worked in the Castle. These were the mystery people who had taken care of everything for me while I was there. They cooked, cleaned, and ran the business of the Castle without me needing to do anything at all. I thanked each one the best that I could. They thanked me for being so brave. I smiled as if I knew what they were talking about because brave was not the feeling that I was having.

In fact, the more they thanked me, the scarier it got. By the time we were done, I understood why Beru had held my hand. I could feel her encouragement flowing through me, and that helped me smile, bow, and say, "Thank you. I'll do my best," to each person I met. It was apparent that they all knew a secret that I didn't know, because there was no way that I would be able to fight the Shrieks and Shatterskin, even with all the help in the world. The thought came that perhaps they were really saying goodbye to me. It wasn't inconceivable. I had no idea how I would survive the Riff.

After the introducing, the amazing food, and the dancing, Beru took me back to my room. I had come to love that room. I was no longer locked in at night, but instead had been taught how to weave an illusion around the door so that no one could see it except the people I trusted.

I had taught Zeid how to high-five, which everyone thought was silly but fun, so the day I hid something from Professor

Link, Zeid high-fived me. I wasn't sure which part was the best—the learning of the skill or that I was learning it with Zeid.

Even Link had nodded at me in approval. My magic making skills were improving. But I didn't believe they were even close to what I would need at the Riff.

As I gazed longingly at my bed, Beru dressed me for the ceremony. Since arriving at the castle, I had been provided clean clothes every day. Although the colors changed, the style stayed pretty much the same. Soft and very durable leggings and a top that draped enough to be comfortable but tight enough not to catch on anything. My clothes had survived multiple falls and slides across the training floor without tearing or ripping. My top had even snagged a knife blade when Niko was showing me how to use a knife, and it didn't tear. Instead, the knife slid off. Very handy for a fairly clumsy and a not very talented fighter like me. I could see Niko shake his head sometimes after another spectacular failure on my part in a sparring match with Zeid.

Once I heard Niko tell Professor Link that he hoped what I was learning in Link's class would save me because my fighting skills sucked. Yes. He used that word. I held no grudges. He was correct.

For the ceremony, Beru gave me a fresh set of clothes and then went to the closet and pulled out a coat I had never seen before. "You'll be needing this," she said. I slipped it on. Like the leggings and top, it was lightweight and fit perfectly.

Then she handed me a backpack filled with who knew what. "You'll need this too, Hannah," she said. After she and I walked out the door, she turned and locked the door. This time I was on the outside.

"Will I ever be back here, Beru?" I asked.

"And you think I know the future, Hannah? I don't. So my

answer is, perhaps yes, perhaps no. What I do know is that after tonight you might not want to return."

It was those words that kept running through my head as we walked through the forest. I could see a fire burning in the distance. The moon lay low on the horizon, lighting our paths. The trees rustled in a breeze that I couldn't feel, their leaves nearing the end of this year's cycle.

Although the path should have been littered with fall leaves, it was as smooth and clear as a walk down the aisle of a church. *Who cleared the path?* I wondered.

When I heard the words, "We did," I had no idea who had spoken. Just as I had no idea what lay before me. But a sense of purpose had infused me from the moment Beru slipped the coat over my shoulder. I was ready.

Twenty-Two

Five minutes later, Beru and I broke through the forest into the clearing. A fire was roaring in the center of a ring of stones. There were five Ginete that I could see standing in the shadows outside of the clearing.

Beru whispered to me, "They have prepared the space for the ceremony and will keep the doors open for you to remember."

I nodded as if I understood. But it was a sense of comfort to see the Ginete in the shadows, arms folded, all-seeing eyes taking in everything. It looked as if they weren't doing anything, but I knew that this ceremony was happening because they agreed to it.

I nodded in their direction, hoping to say thank you, but they avoided my gaze.

I could see Niko, Aki, Suzanne, Zeid, and Ruta seated around the fire. Shadowy figures were sitting in the circle too, but I couldn't make out their faces, and I had no idea who they were. There was an open space in the ring where Beru and I settled in. Nothing was said.

One of the shadows rose, and I saw that it was Professor Link. He walked around the circle putting a small bowl in each of our hands. It was only when he was halfway around the circle that I realized he wasn't carrying the bowls. They appeared in his hands as he gave them to each person, including the shadows.

I was last. The bowl was empty. Professor Link turned and walked the circle again placing something in each bowl. Once again there was nothing in his hands until right before he put it in each bowl. I tried to see what he was doing, but Beru did her famous pinch me in the leg, and I got the message to stop looking.

Everyone was silent, staring into the fire, except for Ruta who was staring at me. When I looked back at him, he gave me one of his stern looks that I had come to fear. Don't cross Ruta. The effects from whatever he had been drinking seemed to have worn off. He was back to his grumpy self.

But now I knew that there was the heart of a dancer beating inside that stump body. I knew I wasn't supposed to be looking at him, but I still gave him the best smile I could muster and I swear I saw his eyebrow rise in recognition and a twinkle in his eye.

By then Link was almost to my bowl, so I turned my attention back to the fire. I stilled my thoughts as best I could. I knew Link would know what was going on inside of me, so I did my best to match what he might be expecting.

Professor Link dropped what looked like shredded tobacco into my bowl and stepped into the fire. Not kidding. Into the fire. No one seemed surprised. I wanted to run and grab him to safety, but when I looked again, I realized that he was untouched. Instead, he looked surprisingly at peace.

He reached out and picked a single flame from the fire, mumbled something and a flame appeared in the center of all our bowls. Luckily I was frozen in place watching Link, so I didn't flinch. Like everyone else I held the bowl steady and didn't put it down until I saw everyone else put their bowl on the ground in front of them.

A sweet, pungent smell was coming from whatever was burning in the bowls, and within a few minutes, the entire campsite was wreathed in smoke.

Still standing in the fire, the professor raised his arms and began to chant. I could feel the heat rising within me. Within seconds I was drenched in sweat. Everything around me faded away.

I closed my eyes and was somewhere else. There were voices all around me. I thought I recognized them, but couldn't remember their names. There was laughter and sobbing. Thunder boomed, and a lightning flash lit up the room where I was standing. I looked out a window at the coming storm. Trees filled in all that I could see. I heard someone say, "But she isn't safe here," then sobbing. Was it me crying?

A soft voice assured me that I would be fine. I wouldn't remember much so I could be happy where I was going. "But what about you?" I heard myself ask. There was no answer. I waited in the silence.

One of the shadows rose and stood before me. "You have returned. We will be waiting for you. Gather your strength. Trust your heritage and the friends that have come to be with you."

Another shadow rose and stood beside the first one. They held hands, bowed, and were gone. I heard sobbing again, and this time I knew it was me. I opened my eyes. The fire had died down to embers. Professor Link was no longer there. The shadows that had been in the circle were gone.

Beru rose and stood in front of me. "Shall I speak your name now?"

Mutely, I nodded.

Beru bowed and said, "Welcome home, Princess Kara Beth."

When I stood up all my friends stood too. "Have you all known who I am?"

When no one answered, I had my answer. Yes, they had known and had waited for me to remember. To return. To protect the kingdom from the man who threatened to destroy everything in his path. I remembered Abbadon and his monsters. And I was mad.

"Do you want to know our plan, Princess Kara Beth?"

"I do. But first I don't want to be called Princess Kara Beth or even Kara. Please call me Hannah. Someday I may return to the name you have given me. But for now, I am Hannah."

I looked around. "I don't remember everything. I'm afraid because I still don't have a memory of any powers I might have once had. I also don't know if all of you were here with me before."

"Your parents thought it best to have you forget while you lived in the Earth dimension, Hannah," Suzanna said.

"It may take time for your powers and your memory to return to you, but we trust that it will. Plus you have your lifetimes in the Earth dimension that will help. You have learned ways of seeing things that we might not see because we have been here, surviving, waiting for the right time to bring you back and fight," Niko said.

I turned to Zeid. "Did I know you before?"

It must have been a strange question to ask because I saw everyone glance at each other before Zeid answered. "You did. But that's not important at this time. Now we must be going."

With one last glance at Zeid, thinking of all the things he might not be telling me, I answered. "So be it. Let's go."

To Beru, I whispered, "Where are we going?"

I might have remembered that I used to live in Erda, and know that I used to be royalty, but for the most part, I was still the clueless person I was before the ceremony. I hoped that would change soon, but in the meantime, I was going to have to count on Beru to get me through it.

"And me," I heard a tiny voice whisper.

I looked down and saw a little face peeking out of my coat pocket. "Now, who are you?" I asked.

And then I remembered.

Twenty-Three

"Pris!" I yelled as I snatched my friend from my pocket.

"Stop it!" Pris said as she wiggled in my hand.

But I couldn't stop clutching her. I had never been so happy to see anyone. Still holding her in my fist, I asked, "Are your sisters here?" I was practically yelling at her until Beru put a restraining hand on my arm.

"Whoops," I whispered. "Yes, I must be quiet. Still, are your sisters here too?"

By then I had opened my hand, and Pris was sitting on it smiling at me. She was as beautiful as I remembered. I realized that I didn't know how long I had been away. I remembered two short lifetimes in the Earth dimension. But were there more that I didn't remember? Did Pris look the same because I hadn't been away for long in their time? Or was it because she didn't age?

Either way, she was there, sitting in my hand like old times. When I saw her, I felt as if the door into my past that had begun to open during the ceremony cracked open a little bit further. I remembered playing together.

Pris had her hair in pigtails with tiny bows on the end of each of them. I remembered pulling them and her laughing and flying off. Having Pris as a friend when I was little was like having a live doll with wings. Smart, funny, and very clever. I also recalled getting in a lot of trouble together.

"This is good, that you remember us," Pris said. "Beru wanted to surprise you. But I wasn't sure you would remember me, even after the ceremony. To answer your question, though, yes, they are here too."

Pris waved her hand, and I looked up to see two more tiny fairies heading my way. Cil and La. I remember asking Pris about their names. She had told me that their mother wanted to be able to call "Priscilla," and they would all come. Most people couldn't tell them apart. But I could. Pris was the oldest sister and had a tiny birthmark that looked like a star on her forehead. Cil was the only one with green eyes, and La's hair had one streak of white in the front.

The sisters landed on each shoulder and kissed my cheek. I couldn't help it. My eyes overflowed. They both giggled and flicked off the tears at their older sister. Just like old times.

"Thank you, Beru," I said.

"I thought you could use their company. Besides, they were driving everyone crazy wanting to see you. And now that they're here, it's time for us to leave. We have a long way to travel, and a few stops to make."

The three sisters tucked into my pockets ready to travel. As much as they like flying, they love being attached to someone and riding along more. I could hear them humming in my pocket, and my heart was happy in spite of the danger that lay ahead.

"What stops? And I don't see Suzanne. Isn't she going with us?" I asked.

"She went ahead. We need to collect your army, don't we?" Beru said with a huff. "Look around you. As wonderful as we all are, do you think we can defeat the Shrieks and Shatterskin by ourselves? Get a grip, let's go. Stop gibber jabbing and start walking."

If Beru had talked to me like that a month before I probably would have started to cry. This time I knew what she was doing. She was hiding how afraid she was for all of us, especially for me. I knew she had been assigned to me by Earl. But I also knew she cared for me, the same way I cared for her. There was no way I was going to let anything happen to her.

As I looked around, I realized that I was not going to let anything happen to any of them. I had no idea how I was going to defeat Abbadon's monsters. But I knew we could do it. Somehow. We'd figure it out. If we needed an army, then I was ready to get them. But I thought that there could be another way. Something kept flashing in the back of my mind. It would come to me.

I just hoped it would come to me in time.

The moon lit the way as Ruta led us through the forest. I knew now that the forest responded to Ruta. I knew that somehow everything moved to make a clear path for him, and therefore for us, so of course he would go first. The rest of us followed.

Beru darted in and out of the forest, never losing sight of our little band, and always making sure that I knew where she was at all times. She was hard to see in the trees unless you knew what to look for. Aki walked with Ruta, and Niko was behind all of us. Up ahead I could hear Lady drumming. She was scouting ahead of us, sending back signals about which way to go,

My friends walked together as if they had done this before many times. They were a team. I could see that now. Trained, alert, and prepared. I wondered how long they had waited for me to come back. The list of questions that I had kept stacking up.

During my squealing with happiness fit when I saw Pris and her sisters, Zeid had stood aside and watched with a tiny smile on his lips. As we started moving, Zeid moved up to walk beside me. He didn't say anything, but I could tell something was on his mind. Something had happened during the ceremony, or more accurately, something hadn't happened that upset him.

Perhaps he expected me to remember him and was disappointed that I didn't. If I were in his shoes, I would be disappointed too. Still, he walked beside me, and I knew he was there because he wanted to be and he would protect me no matter what. I just didn't know why.

Twenty-Four

"Why don't we ride in the bubble?" I asked Beru.

I was already tired of walking. We had stopped to rest by a stream to fill our water containers and eat. Judging from the sun, since there were no watches, I figured we'd been walking steadily for at least five hours.

How much further could it be? Besides if there was magic everywhere why weren't we using it? It seemed like a reasonable question to me, but Beru gave me a look that would have stunned a bird off its branch.

Apparently, my question wasn't worth answering because she stormed off to sit beside Ruta. The Priscillas had popped themselves out of my pocket and sat sunning themselves on a rock while snacking on sunflower seeds. Cil had flown off and returned with them to share with her sisters.

Who knew how she found sunflowers in a forest, but if anyone could find food it was fairies. They had to have a nose for food. As tiny as they were they had to eat a lot, to keep their energy flowing. It reminded me of hummingbirds back home. Maybe it was hummingbirds in the Earth dimension and fairies in Erda? I added it to my growing list of questions.

The rest of us were sitting in a circle eating food we had

packed in our backpacks. Well, I didn't pack mine. Beru must have done it before handing it to me. I snuck a look over at her sitting with her back to me talking to Ruta about something. Maybe she had a right to be angry with me. I was complaining even when so much had been done for me. But magic was to be used, right?

"Wrong," Niko said. "Wrong thinking. Stupid thinking. Selfish thinking."

Aki and Niko hadn't said a word to me since the ceremony, so I was startled by him sitting beside me, the fact he was reading my thoughts willy-nilly, and by what he said. Niko was always short on words, and always abrupt, so maybe I shouldn't have been. But, hadn't I learned anything? People were still reading my mind, and my feelings were still getting hurt.

"You'll never be able to totally block any of us, Hannah," Niko said. "You might not like it, but for now it's for your own protection. Think of it like any of the protective forces you know from the Earth dimension, like the police or military. They wear devices to communicate with each other. We don't need physical devices to communicate. Just as we don't need most of the physical equipment you are used to using. We have harnessed energy differently.

"As for using magic to get a ride. No. Not done. We are not wasteful. We don't abuse the gift we have been given. If there is a reason to use magic we will. Not until then."

Taking advantage of Niko's talking spree, I decided to ask him more questions. I could ponder what he had said as we walked. Didn't like it, but I sort of, kind of, understood.

"May I ask, please, Niko, how long we will be walking today and where we are going."

"Today we will walk until twilight. Use the time wisely. Think. Practice your fighting skills in your head. Look around you. Listen. You are not a little girl anymore, Hannah. You are Princess Kara Beth whether you like it or not. Remember yourself, because if you survive, someday you will be Queen Kara Beth. And if you don't survive, neither does this world. Grow up, Hannah."

Niko walked away and turned his back on me the same way that Beru had done.

Everyone had heard. I was mortified. I wanted to get up and stomp off. I wanted a door to slam. I wanted to cry, yell, run away. Instead, I sat on my rock and stared straight ahead. Grow up. Right. Easy to say. But I knew he was right. I was whining. No one else was, and for some reason, their fate rested in my hands. They didn't ask for this either.

No one said anything. It felt as if the entire forest had sucked in its breath and was waiting. Even the birds were silent. There was nothing for me to say except, "I'm sorry."

The forest let out its breath, and everyone returned to eating and murmuring with each other. The Priscillas flew to my head and attached themselves to my hair. If they did it the right way, they looked like decorations. La leaned down and whispered in my ear. "Everything will be okay, Hannah."

Simple words that spun through me washing away my frustration and revealing that tiny flame of purpose I had felt before, back in the Castle. I whispered back, "Thank you." I lifted my head to the sun and let its presence fill me with renewed energy. Closing my eyes, I did a short meditation that Aki had taught me.

I could feel the warmth of the sun, so it was easy to imagine light moving through me, filling me, dropping down into the earth and rising into the sky. I imagined the light moving out into an ever-widening circle surrounding my team and me with its power and protection.

The rock that I was sitting on wasn't solid anymore. It was a living, breathing being. Underneath it, I could sense tree roots connecting in a mass of intertwining fibers. They too were breathing. Everything was breathing. The world was breathing.

One last light pulse and the image was gone. My eyes flew open, and I looked around. The world looked the same as it did before. What was that? Was I going crazy?

Niko and Beru were no longer sitting with their backs to me. Everyone was smiling at me. Well, if I was crazy, then they were too. Might as well go with it. Besides, I felt the difference in myself. I felt supported. Not tired at all. The flame was still there, burning a little brighter than before.

Niko gave me a nod. I had done something right. I corrected myself. I had gotten out of the way and allowed something to happen.

I heard Lady's drumming in the distance. This time I knew what she was saying. The coast was clear. It was time to move on. It was only after we had been walking another few hours that I realized that Niko had never told me where we were going.

It pleased me that the need to know had faded. That thought must have pleased Niko too because I heard him say in my head. "Well done, Hannah."

Twenty-Five

Niko was true to his word. We stopped at twilight. Everyone helped gather downed branches and logs from the forest floor. When we had enough wood, Beru held her hand out and started the fire, as easily as she had put it out before, right after I came through the portal. A million years ago. Or so it felt. I still had a bit of homesickness in my stomach, but it was fading, like a dream. I could sense the memories in the back of my mind, but details were blurry.

Watching Beru starting and stopping fires, I wanted to do what looked like magic as effortlessly as she did, as they all did. Like Ruta clearing a path through the trees, or Aki levitating, or Suzanne appearing and disappearing. I realized that I had accepted them as part of my day. Magic as a way of being. And yet, I didn't have any magic, let alone effortless magic. Or, if I did, it hadn't appeared. I hoped I found it before it was too late.

While we ate, Ruta was making trips in and out of the woods with what looked like logs, but he laid them in a circle around the fire rather than putting them in. I was too hungry to be more than slightly curious. Beru had produced bars out of my pack, and I was so used to her providing for me I didn't bother to ask her how she kept doing that. Niko had filled all our water pouches, but I didn't know where he had gotten the water. We had moved away from the stream. And again there were rocks to sit on, and I wondered how there were always rocks where we needed them.

Back in the Earth dimension, all of this would have been extraordinary. Here, in Erda it was common. Or so it seemed.

"You're right about that, Hannah," Zeid said sitting beside me. "And yet you're wrong about that too."

"Zounds, Zeid, you keep doing that. You keep sneaking up on me! Cut it out! And stop listening in on my thinking, for ziffer's sake."

Zeid laughed at me. "If you would pay attention, you would see me coming. Don't you think that is part of what you need to learn? I'm not dangerous when I sneak up on you, but other people and beings will be. As for reading your mind, stop leaving it wide open to people like me."

"People like you? What kind of person are you? Mind reader? And what did you mean I was right and I was wrong."

"You're right. It is common among us." Zeid looked around the circle. "Our little crew has been gathered precisely for their skills. Each member has spent years honing their art. It's second nature to them.

"However, you're wrong, because outside of these friends magic is a dying art. People have stopped practicing it. Many people have become complacent. They use their skills just enough to provide for themselves and have a decent life. They remain apathetic to the danger of losing their abilities."

"So everyone in Erda has magical skills, they just don't use them?"

"Of course. Look around. Nature provides everything. It's the visible expression of life that holds the earth together. Energy, force, doesn't matter what you call it, it's all around. In you. Around you. In everyone and around everyone.

"There's more than one reason why we are walking, Hannah. You are here to learn. To reconnect. To find yourself." Zeid's eyes burned into me as if his passion for what he was saying could somehow connect me to my skills.

I looked away, barely able to handle what he was saying. If it was around and in me, why couldn't I feel it yet?

"Look, Hannah. You have to stop worrying about it. Part of using the magic within and finding your specific talent, is letting go and trusting. It's a mindset. You are Princess Kara Beth. You have used your skills in the past. They haven't gone anywhere."

"People keep reminding me that I am a zonking princess as if that will help. It just makes me feel worse."

Zeid shook his head. "Sometimes, Hannah, you disappoint me. But I do believe that we are on a mission that will succeed. It has to. Abbadon will destroy all that you see if we don't. Without us stopping him, he will kill everyone. He wants to be the only person in Erda with magic skills. He wants to rule all of Erda. There is no way that we can allow evil to be the winner here. And Abbadon is the king of evil.

"We will succeed. You will step up and be who you are. I know that you will, Hannah."

As Zeid moved away, I thought that he was dangerous, to me anyway. I tried not to notice how he looked at me and how that felt. Sometimes I could feel his azure eyes staring at me when he didn't think I was paying attention. I paid too much attention to him, that was the problem. I couldn't let myself feel anything for him. It made me feel disloyal to Johnny. That boy was fading in my dreams and Zeid was not helping. Zeid was wrong. He is dangerous.

Zeid's back flinched, and I prayed that he hadn't heard that series of thoughts. But the flinch made me think that perhaps he did, and now I was in even more trouble than before. Zut. I had to stop this craziness.

But his disappointment in me, and his belief in me, fueled my desire to find my talents. I didn't have to make them. I just had to let myself return to them. I had returned to Erda. I could return to being who I was before.

By then it was time to sleep for the night. Niko had first watch. I was not on the watch list, and I knew why. I would be less than useless.

It turned out the logs that Ruta had pulled out of the woods weren't logs at all. They were mats of moss rolled up like a yoga mat. Beru was already on her mat, and she patted the one beside her for me.

The Priscillas had been quiet the whole time Zeid had been talking to me, but now they started a soothing hum while Beru threw a gathering of leaves on top of me. It was almost as comfortable as my bed back home. "Which home?" I asked myself as I fell asleep. It surprised me to realize that I was thinking of the Castle as home.

Twenty-Six

We were up before dawn and were already moving out as the sun peeked up over the horizon, splitting its rays between the trees. Finally, I had become aware enough to notice we had our backs to the rising sun. We were moving west. Was it possible that the portal that opened in Erda had been close to where my home was in the Earth dimension?

That was something I had neglected to ask, and now I wanted to know. When Beru answered in my head that I was correct, this time I was delighted that she had been listening. It was an intriguing thought that the portal had been near my home all along.

When Beru projected an image of an open meadow to me, I knew where it was. It was a meadow on a hillside ringed with trees. That meadow had been both a happy and a sad place for me in my Earth life. It was also strange to think of my life as divided between my Earth life and my Erda life. Earth was then. Erda was now.

When no one corrected me, I knew I was right. I might never go home again. And even if I did, it wouldn't be the same. "Unless we wipe your memory, Hannah," Beru said. "And we would never do that unless all is lost here. Then we would send you back to the Earth Realm to be safe. Otherwise, we will not be opening any portal anywhere again until Abbadon is defeated, or it becomes absolutely necessary."

The Priscillas on my coat twittered in concern. I reached down and gently pulled Pris's pigtail. It was the best I could do right then to reassure her.

As we walked, I kept feeling a presence walking beside me on the left. But every time I looked, nothing was there. Whatever the presence was, it felt dangerous, but not to me. I was attempting to practice awareness when I caught a glimpse of something.

"Beru, there is something here beside me." I didn't say that out loud. I knew that she, and everyone else, was listening in on our common channel.

"Sure is," was the response.

"That's it? Sure is? What is it? How come you didn't tell me?"

"Why do you think? You have got to see these things for yourself. Besides he has been waiting a long time for you to see him. You have to choose to see him."

"Him? Long time? How long?"

"Since you returned to Erda. He waited in the forest outside the Castle."

I felt like bopping Beru on the head. Ruta had fashioned a beautiful walking stick for me, and it felt like the perfect thing to use. But I didn't dare. What would she do in return?

"Oh, for zut's sake, Hannah, stop complaining and open up." That was Ruta of course. Mr. Grump. But he was right.

I turned my thoughts to the presence walking beside me and addressed it specifically, doing my best to turn off the open channel to everyone else.

"At least I feel you," I said. "I'm ready to see you now."

Nothing happened. I tried again. "Seriously, I am ready.

Show yourself to me."

I heard a loud growl. I screamed and stopped in my tracks, dropping my walking stick in the process. Yep, that's me. The ready to fight at a moment's notice machine. I was weaponless and scared out of my mind.

In front of me sat the most massive wolf I had ever seen. Well, I had never seen a live wolf before, so I imagined it was bigger than most wolves. Actually, I wasn't even sure if it was a wolf. But it looked like pictures I had seen. It was baring its teeth at me. Its piercing gold eyes were locked on me. I was a goner.

I was too frozen to move. Was I supposed to run? Fight? Use my nonexistent magic? Why wasn't anyone coming to my rescue? Didn't they know there was a wolf in front of me ready to attack?

The next thing I knew Zeid was beside me. "Are you disappointing me again, Hannah?"

He started walking towards the wolf. "Wait, wait!" I yelled after him and then stopped in embarrassment. Zeid was patting that monster on the head.

"Please, just open the earth and let me drop through it," I said to whoever was listening.

"Get your lazy, fraidy-cat ass over here, Hannah," Zeid commanded.

Gathering up my courage, I walked forward. The closer I got to the monster wolf, the more a feeling of deep contentment and love started rolling over me. And the door to my past opened a little bit further.

"Cahir," I cried throwing my arms around the wolf and burying my face in his neck.

Memories of our time together rolled through my mind. Cahir as a pup. His mother delivering him to me personally.

Her gift to me. Her precious son, Cahir, a warrior, to stand by me. I sobbed into his fur as he stood waiting for me as he always had.

Cahir and I didn't share words. We shared images. I saw his life without me while he waited for my return. He hadn't aged. Like most beings in Erda, age was chosen. Although there were children, once any being reached the age that they felt was the perfect age for them, their aging slowed dramatically. That stop age was different for everyone.

Cahir had been almost at his prime when I left. He had chosen to stop there as he waited. While I was gone he aged just enough to be at his prime now. That's what he showed me. How he had prepared for my return. He showed me the family he had now. A pack of wolves. A wife, and pups.

"But you are traveling alone," I whispered to him. His reply was to show his family safe in another place. Shadows of people were around them. I recognized seeing those shadows before, but still didn't know who they were or where they were.

"You will, when it's time," Zeid said.

This time instead of being mad at him for listening in, I looked up and smiled at him. I watched as a look of shock and then pleasure passed through him before he smiled back.

Cahir and Zeid were friends that told me what I had wanted to know. Something I hadn't realized I was wondering. Could I trust Zeid or not? Now I knew that I could, and that changed so many things for me.

"Move out, we have a long way to go," Niko said. Up ahead, Lady drummed as she scouted for a safe way for us to travel.

Zeid fell into step beside me, and this time I saw Cahir on my left. With the two of them walking with me I felt better than I had in a long time.

Twenty-Seven

I could hear Niko and Ruta talking, but I couldn't understand what they were saying. They had blocked their minds from me which meant I had to know.

La knew what I wanted, so she flew up to Niko and arranged herself to look like a leaf that had fallen to his coat. The Priscillas abilities to camouflage themselves was going to come in handy. Even if my magical gifts never returned, I did have powerful friends. Now with Cahir by my side, I felt ready to take on whatever we were heading into.

"They were wondering if you would be able to do anything once we reach the village," La said when she returned.

"What village, did they say?"

"I already know where we are going," La replied. "We are stopping at Beru's village to pick up supplies. Didn't she tell you?"

Now that Cahir walked beside me, Beru often walked with Ruta. It was like watching a tree stump walking with a flower—if such a thing could happen.

"No, she didn't. How long until we get there?"

"Keeping to this pace, we'll be there before nightfall, but I doubt we'll all go in at night. Likely they will send a few people up ahead to prepare for our return."

I was puzzled. Why wait? Maybe they had warm houses and soft beds that we could sleep in. The thought made me giddy with happiness.

It was Cil that answered me. "Some people in the village may not like us being there."

When I motioned impatiently for her to go on, she added, "Some people think that Beru is a traitor."

"What! Why?"

"Perhaps that is a tale for someone else to tell," Zeid said breaking into the conversation. He and Cahir took turns walking with me. They also took turns disappearing into the woods. I assumed it was some sort of scouting thing, but neither of them let me in on what they were doing.

"Who is going to tell it? You?"

Our conversation was interrupted as I heard Lady's call and looked up to see her coming toward us. It was an impressive sight. In the Earth dimension, I always thought that pileated woodpeckers looked like miniature dragons. Big birds, tiny dragons.

Here in Erda, Lady had grown. Every time I saw her, she was bigger than the last time. Now, if Lady landed on my head the way she used to in Earth, I would be squashed. As she circled above us, she no longer looked like a miniature dragon. She looked like a dragon. Smaller than the huge ones I used to see pictures of in books, but at least the size of a car in Earth.

Honestly, seeing her circle like that, she scared me. I wondered if she had been a dragon all along. A white and black one with flashes of red, but still a dragon. I also wondered if she breathed fire.

"All that and more," Zeid said.

When I turned to look at him to ask more questions, he

shook his head and pointed. "I think she has decided that you are ready to see this."

Puzzled, I turned back to see that Lady had landed on the ground beside Niko and Aki. As I watched, Lady disappeared, and Suzanne stood in her place. She looked over at me and smiled. Suzanne could have laughed at me instead because I was standing there with my mouth hanging open far enough for a small bird to fly into. I closed my eyes and opened them again. It was still Suzanne.

She walked towards me and hugged me. I remember thinking that it was good she was hugging me as a woman and not a dragon. Her embrace was warm and comforting. I wasn't sure what Lady's would feel like.

Suzanne took me by the·hand and led me over to a nearby rock under the shade of a beautiful old oak. Some of its branches hung so low I could have easily climbed up into the tree. If a tree could listen, it felt as if it was getting ready to enjoy our conversation.

"I thought you were ready to know about this," Suzanne said. "Are you?"

"I think so," I whispered staring at her. She looked like the Erda Suzanne, the one with black leggings, red tunic, and spiked hair. She answered my unspoken question, "Yes, here in Erda I look more like myself. The bird you called Lady in Earth wasn't me. I did use her though, with her permission. I flew with her to see you, but she wasn't a dragon, you see, and I am. The Lady that you saw after you came through the portal with you was me."

"So, you're a shapeshifter? I thought that was a myth."

"In the Earth dimension, shapeshifters have been relegated to myth. Just as what we call magic has been boxed into the phrase paranormal. Out of the normal way of being. Erda has never lost the sense of magic. It isn't out of the normal. It is the normal."

Still trying to take in that Suzanne was also a bird-dragon, I asked, "Are there other shapeshifters in Erda?"

Suzanne took both my hands in hers and said, "There are many things in Erda that you have yet to remember. Perhaps the question of other shapeshifters is something we can discuss at another time. Right now, do you accept that is what I am?"

When I nodded, yes, she continued. "Good. Because we have work to do, and both Suzanne and Lady will be helping you. Tomorrow we'll all be going into Kinvar.

"As you heard, not everyone will be happy to see us, so you will need to be hyper alert. Cahir won't be coming into the village with you. He'll be patrolling the borders while you all are there."

Nodding at everyone, Suzanne stepped away from me and transformed back into a dragon called Lady. If I would have known, I am not sure I would have called her such a refined name. As a dragon, Lady was beautifully terrifying.

"Love my name, Lady," I heard Suzanne say. "Ladies sometimes must be beautifully terrifying to those who attempt to do evil. Something to aspire to, Hannah."

"What?" I asked.

"Be a beautifully terrifying woman. You'll need to be," Lady said as she headed away into the forest. I watched until I couldn't see her anymore.

"You are already beautiful, Hannah," Zeid said.

"But not yet terrifying," Niko added.

I smiled at Zeid and stared at Niko. No, I didn't feel beautiful, but I did like hearing Zeid say that I was.

However, I didn't do anything to be beautiful, but I was willing to become terrifying. Perhaps there was a store where I could buy it.

Everyone laughed. Well, at least people thought I was humorous. Maybe that was a start.

Twenty-Eight

As Cil and La predicted, we didn't go into the village that night. As we sat around the campfire that Beru had brought into existence, I waited for someone to tell me what was going on. Just before I was ready to open my mouth and ask about the village and Beru, Pris pulled my hair and hissed, "Not now. Just wait."

It hurts when a fairy pulls your hair, so I shut up. Okay, I pouted and shut up. To take my mind off of talking, I settled into eating and staring at the fire. We always had food. Somehow. It was as if the food came to us, like the water. We never had leftovers, and everyone had what they liked, or needed to eat. I didn't always know what I was eating, but it always tasted good.

Yes. I knew I was spoiled. People took care of me all of the time. As we walked, Niko would have me practicing some of the moves that he had taught me back at the Castle.

Aki gave me walking meditation exercises to do, and I thought that my awareness of what was around me was improving. Then one of them would sneak up on me, and I knew I was still failing.

Beru told me that I had to trust that my skills would return.

As Princess Kara Beth I had been considered a powerful mage. Right.

"Snap out of it, Hannah," Pris hissed again. "If you keep on letting yourself fall into that poor-me point of view you are worse than useless. Besides, Beru is ready."

I looked up and saw that Beru was standing beside Ruta waiting for me to notice. Everyone was. My face turned bright red but I caught myself before I started falling into my mode of beating myself up. Actually, it was Pris looking right into my eyes that stopped me from descending into my pity party. Her little tiny wings were flapping furiously, and her face could have halted a wall of water.

Once Beru saw that she had my attention she began. She told us that the village we had come to was the village where most of her family still lived and had lived for thousands of years. They had been content. Like most beings in Erda, they lived a long time after the age where they stopped growing. She reminded me that beings in Erda didn't die from old age. They died if they were killed, an accident occurred, or they chose to move on.

Beru had family that had lived for perhaps a thousand years. No one counted years in Erda as it wasn't important. What was important was how well they lived in harmony with each other and with the land.

That was true not just for her village but for all of the Erda dimension where Abbadon didn't rule, which for a long time was most of the planet. However, Abbadon was never content. He always wanted more, so he began to extend his rule past his homeland.

Rumors of Abbadon's reign of destruction had come to the village, but no one took them seriously. Life was too good. The little magic they practiced provided for a happy life. However, hearing the rumors, Beru had grown discontent. She often wandered past the village grounds into the forest where she met Ruta. He too had become worried because of the rumors, even though his people also did not believe them. They often walked the woods together and discussed what they had heard about Abbadon.

When they were in their youth, Beru and Ruta had heard about the Evil One who lived to the west. However, Abbadon was considered a fairy tale, a myth, not a reality. Not a threat.

Ruta and Beru often walked for days to see what the rest of their world was like. No one worried when they were gone, because no one believed in an Evil One. Besides, Beru and Ruta were hundreds of years old and had much-accumulated wisdom between the two of them.

One day they had walked so far they reached mountains far to the west of their home. After debating whether or not to climb the mountain, they decided to give it a try. After all, they reasoned, they would probably never come this way again.

What they found when they reached the top was so terrifying they couldn't take it in at first. Far into the distance, past the forest that spilled down the mountain and across the valley, Ruta and Beru saw emptiness. No trees. None as far as their eyes could see. Only a barren, brown, and broken landscape.

A pair of Hawks had landed behind them in the trees and gave Ruta and Beru permission to see with their eyes. Using animals and birds to see something was a form of magic rarely practiced, and neither Ruta or Beru knew how to do it. But with the Hawks' guidance, they mentally entered into the Hawks' minds and saw the world as a Hawk sees it. What the Hawks showed them was more terrifying than words could describe.

At this point in the story, Beru sat down, clearly still upset by what they found, and Ruta took over. His grumpiness was gone as he gave the account of what the birds had shown them.

Not only was the land brown and barren, it was shattered. It was as if a giant hand had reached down and grabbed handfuls of the earth and flung it everywhere. Trees were blown apart, their roots waving in the air. Every rock was a tiny fragment. The wind swirled dust tornadoes. The dust was often so dense the Hawks often had to rise above it to find their way.

When the view was clear, the Hawks had swooped down close to the ground and showed them green blobs moving between the shattered land and into the forest. They were making a shrieking sound that seemed to stun everything around them. There was a moment of panic when one of the Shrieks noticed them, and the Hawks rose quickly and returned to where Beru and Ruta stood at the top of the mountain.

Once their eyes were released, the Hawks told them what the Shrieks did. Many birds had died, fallen from the sky before they realized that they could rise higher than the sound. The animals were not so lucky. The Shrieks would stun them, and Shatterskin would literally shatter the ground, and every living thing. It was always total destruction wherever they went, and they were moving East taking the land bit by bit.

I realized that Ruta was telling the story for me. This team of people knew this story. But even though they knew it already and had probably witnessed the destruction first hand, I saw tears hanging in almost everyone's eyes.

"What happened then? Is this how you all came together?" I asked.

"In time," Niko answered. "Yes, there is more to this story. But the important part for today is that Beru and Ruta returned to their villages and told them what they had seen.

"Sadly, not only were they not believed, they were shunned."

Twenty-Nine

After that story, Niko and Aki headed down into the village to let them know that we were coming.

Ruta and Beru left the fire and settled down onto their moss mats without saying another word. I couldn't blame them. What more was there to tell that could have made it better? That meant it was only me, the Priscillas, and Zeid sitting by the fire. Cahir was in the woods, patrolling. I knew Lady was there too. I could hear her drumming leading Niko and Aki safely to the village.

For once, I was speechless. Shunned? What would that feel like? The people that you love stop talking to you. You become invisible to them? All because Ruta and Beru were trying to bring them a warning about what was coming? It was a classic story though. Even in my Earth home, there were those warning about more than meets the eye and coming dangers. There was the fable about Plato's cave and the story of Cassandra. They too were ignored and mistreated.

I could understand that first reaction. I didn't want to hear about Evil or its coming, either. But at least I knew that pretending it wasn't there was never going to make it go away.

I thought back through the Cain and Abel story that Aki

had told me that day back in the Castle. I understood that Cain was Abbadon. However, she never told me who Abel was in Erda.

"I wondered when you would get around to that, Hannah," Zeid said.

I gave Zeid one of the faces I had been practicing after watching Pris, the master of making faces. It didn't appear to work. He laughed instead.

"Okay. You win," I said. "I didn't think of asking before, and maybe I should have, but now I am. Who is the Abel in Erda?"

"Well," Zeid said, getting serious, "It's an important question. And it really wasn't your fault that you didn't ask. Aki blocked you from thinking about it because she didn't think you were ready to hear it."

"Ziffer, zut, zounds," I said, "What is this with you all? I'm not ready? Here I am getting ready to fight Shrieks and Shatterskin, and I still don't know everything? When will I be ready then? When Shatterskin blows us all apart, and as our pieces scatter over the planet, one of you says, 'Oops, sorry, forgot to tell you.'"

Zeid turned to me and took me by the shoulders and shook me. The Priscillas clung to my coat. Pris buried her head under the collar. I couldn't blame her. Zeid's face looked like thunder. A part of me tried to see how he made that face. It was very effective. The rest of me was a bit terrified.

A moment later I realized why he was angry, and he had a right to be. They were working hard to save Erda in general, and me specifically, and I was acting like a brat once again.

My awareness must have shown because he let me go and turned back to the fire.

"You are going to have to trust us, Hannah. We've been here in Erda the whole time. You've been gone. You've lost most of your memory of Erda, and not recovered your magical talents. We didn't know that would happen when we sent you away. We thought you'd remember and that it wouldn't take time to return to yourself.

"We learned that we were wrong about that when the people you call the Forest Circle returned. It took time. Except for Suzanne and her father, Earl. They had been continually traveling between dimensions, instead of living just in Earth, so they never forgot. But those that we sent away to live in Earth did forget because we wanted them to, not realizing that they wouldn't remember when they came back. When they returned, it has taken them varying degrees of time to remember and to recover.

"That's why we have taken so much time to reintroduce you to Erda. But Shatterskin is still marching East, and we can't wait any longer."

"Who else did you send away, Zeid?" I demanded. "The ones that forgot. And why them. And why me?"

"You haven't figured that out, Hannah?" Jake answered

"Because I am Princess Kara Beth?"

"And that means someday you might be what, Hannah?"

"Queen? Queen of what?"

Zeid waved his hand to take in our surroundings. "This, Hannah. All of this is your land. You are the daughter of the other brother. You will be Queen if he dies, or if he chooses to turn it all over to you. That is if we can save the planet from Abbadon. Otherwise, there will be no Kingdom left, and no beings of any kind for you to take care of.

"You were sent away, which for us was a brief span of time. We didn't know if Abbadon would target you first, so we did what we thought was best. Maybe we were wrong, given the outcome, but there is nothing we can do now."

Zeid rose to go, and I grabbed his hand. "You haven't told me yet, Zeid. Who are my mother and father? Where are they? "

Zeid turned and knelt in front of me. The look of sadness on his face scared me. "Your mother is dead, Hannah. She was visiting one of the villages in the West when the Shrieks arrived. Everyone died. There were no survivors. The entire town was stunned, and then shattered and swallowed. Buried. That's why your father, in his grief, sent you away to be safe."

"And my father?"

"Survives. But his grief has weighed him down, and he is dying from it."

"Does he know I have returned?"

"Yes. At least part of him knows. The part that has given up does not, and that's the part that governs him right now. Once we have defeated the Shrieks and Shatterskin we'll go to see him, and hopefully, he will recover because you have returned. If we don't, it won't make any difference anyway."

This time I didn't stop Zeid from walking away. My world was shattered once again. All along I realized that I had harbored the belief that Leif and Sarah might be my birth parents. Now I knew they were not. My mother was dead. My father was dying, and I still didn't remember them. I didn't even know their names.

I looked down at the Priscillas in my lap. "You know who they are don't you."

They all looked down at their hands trying not to make eye contact with me.

"Please," I said. "At least tell me their names. Perhaps it will help me remember."

Pris looked up and sighed.

"My parent's names, please?"

"Rowena and Darius."

I hoped their names would open the door further into my memory, but nothing happened.

I don't know how long I remained staring into the fire until the Priscillas talked me into lying down, reminding me that the next day we would be going into Beru's village. I would need my rest.

"Give it time," Pris said, as I lay on my moss mat. The three of them hummed until I fell asleep, hoping I would dream of my parents.

Thirty

If I dreamed, I didn't remember. I probably didn't have time enough to dream because Niko and Aki woke us all in the middle of the night and told us that we had to go. No one asked why. For once I kept my mouth shut and did what I was told to do.

Cahir came to my side, and we were off through the woods. As always, we had a safe path, provided by Ruta and the trees. A path that closed behind us as we walked. We could see where we were going because there was a faint light coming from the ground. As soon as we passed, the light faded away.

I had seen this phenomenon before, so I wasn't surprised, but this time as I walked I could feel the energy coming from the ground through the soles of my feet. When I bent down to touch the earth, I could feel a slight vibration. It was like the breath I had felt when I had the dream of the planet breathing in and out.

When I stood, Zeid smiled at me. He must have sensed what I had felt. There was nothing to say. Something had clicked back on. It was a good sign, one that we both needed.

Without speaking out loud, I asked Pris where we were going.

"The village," was her answer. I knew there wouldn't be any more explanation, so I let it rest.

As we crested the hill, the village of Kinver appeared below. The sun had just risen and was painting the roofs of the buildings a soft pink. I could see what looked like the main street of maybe ten stores, and a few roads that fanned from there. It didn't seem larger than maybe one hundred buildings.

The closer we got, the prettier it looked. Kinver was filled with gardens of all kinds. Although it was fall, there was enough left in each plot to see that there were both flowers and vegetables in the mix.

Once we reached the road into town, I could see two groups of people facing each other. In the middle was a man who appeared to be keeping them on their respective sides.

"What's going on?" I asked Niko.

"Now, Hannah, what does it look like to you?"

"Disagreement."

"And so it is. Now we need to resolve it. And that, my dear, will be up to you."

I stopped in my tracks. "Wait. What are you talking about? I don't know these people. I don't know what to say to them."

Niko turned and looked at me the same way he looked when he sent me out to spar with Zeid.

"They know you, Princess Kara Beth. They don't know that you don't remember them. They know your ability. They trust you. They will follow you. We have told them what Beru and Ruta warned them about is true. We scared the living crap out of them. Or I hope we did.

"But they are still not sure. The villagers think that if they stay here, they will be safe. The Shrieks and Shatterskin are far away. They don't believe that they will ever come this far East.

"You, Kara Beth, have to convince them to do two things:

fortify their town, and practice their magic skills again. And, you who don't remember enough to be effective, have to convince them that you still have magic, and you need some of them to join us as we head out to destroy the Shrieks."

My blood was boiling. Niko spoke to me as if I were less than nothing. The more he talked, the madder I got. It wasn't my fault I didn't remember anything. I didn't ask to be Princess Whatever. Niko spoke to me as if I was utterly incapable.

No, I didn't remember being any kind of princess, but I did remember being Hannah. Hannah who was more than capable in Earth. Much more than she was in Erda. Hannah who had talents and abilities that changed people's lives. I remembered her.

Niko kept poking at me with words. I felt something happen. Power surged up my legs and out my arm, and I touched Niko with it. He fell on his ass. And laughed.

"Now, that's my girl," he said. "Use that."

Realizing that he had just used me, made me even angrier. So angry I only had a small awareness that my touch had landed my martial arts instructor right on his butt in the middle of the street.

I marched to the front of my team. Yes, my team. I stopped in front of the man who was standing between the two crowds.

One side cheered and bowed to me. The other glared. Perhaps that group of people didn't recognize me. I lifted my hand above my head and sent a bolt of lightning from my hand. It shocked me almost as much as it astonished the crowd. Both sides started cheering as I pretended that I knew what I had done.

I turned slowly, staring at them in turns, giving them a look like the woman they knew would be their queen someday. Powerful. In charge. I thought of the words Suzanne had spoken, "beautifully terrifying," and tried to look that way.

I saw part of my team standing together to the right of me. Niko, Aki, Zeid, Ruta, and Beru. The Priscillas were tucked into my coat pocket. I could see Lady sitting in a huge tree right outside the village, and I knew Cahir was waiting for me on the outskirts of the crowd.

I felt powerful. I knew the fight was for me to do. The team knew it, and now I knew it too. I had remembered enough magic to make the village stop and listen. I had to use the gift of words to convince them to do what needed to be done and to recognize that their daughter and friend, Beru, was a hero.

Standing in front of one of the crowds was a little girl. She was leaning against her mother, and her father had his hand on her shoulder. She was counting on me to keep her and her family safe. I was not about to let her down. When she smiled, I knew that she had not forgotten her magic and was ready to use it. At that moment, we understood each other.

I bowed, planted my walking stick firmly into the ground, and began. And the village listened.

Thirty-One

I found Beru standing in one of the gardens on one of the smaller roads off of the main street. It looked as if it had been neglected for a long time, so I wondered what had brought Beru to it.

After my demonstration of lightning leaping from my hands, and the two crowds becoming one, Niko took over. I'm sure he sensed my desperation. Shooting lightning bolts were enough for me to handle at the time.

By the time Niko was done with them, the village of Kinver was eating out of his hands, both literally and figuratively. First, he convinced them that there was a danger, and it was necessary to protect their village. Pay attention, post scouts, prepare to fight, practice their magic, and cloak the town the best that they could. It wasn't a skill that was often practiced, but Niko promised to give the most gifted among them a how-to lesson before we moved on.

Imagine that. A how-to lesson on how to cloak a village. Not one on how to put up a gutter, or run a program on your computer—a magic lesson. I couldn't get over how cool that was. Maybe I was getting used to being back in Erda while maintaining the wide-eyed wonder I had brought with me from the Earth Realm.

I thought that Niko would collect people to march with us, like an army, but he said that fighting the Shrieks and Shatterskin could not be won by brute force but by outsmarting them. However, a small group of men did volunteer to come with us, and after conferring with Zeid and Aki, he agreed to take them on.

After that, he fed them. All of them. Once again, there was food. A long table was placed in the center of the main street, and everyone was invited. Food of all shapes and sizes was piled on the table by Niko, Aki, and Zeid. No one seemed surprised. Maybe magically appearing food was ordinary, or after seeing lightning bolts shoot into the sky, the villagers were ready for anything.

After taking enough food to satisfy the little hunger that I had, I went off in search of Beru. She had disappeared as soon as Niko began his talk.

It was such a small village it didn't take me long to find her. Beru was standing alone, and either didn't hear me coming, or allowed me to think that she didn't. As I came closer, I could see the tracks of tears on her cheeks. I was surprised. Since I had known her, I had never sensed a trace of sadness, in spite of being shunned. Now that the village had welcomed her again, and she and Ruta were no longer outcasts, she was sad.

"Why the tears, Beru?"

When she didn't answer, I waited and listened which is what I should have done in the first place. In all of the village, I had not seen Beru greet anyone. Where were her parents?

"They aren't here any longer," Beru answered my unspoken question.

"They died?"

Beru turned to me with a slight smile on her beautiful face.

"No. At least I don't think so. After I left, the village didn't treat them well, so they moved. No one is sure where they went. I hope it was further east though, and not to the west."

Usually, Beru didn't like to be hugged, and I am not much of a hugger anyway, but this time I reached out and pulled her close to me. We were about the same height, but she was a wisp compared to me. It was like hugging a flower.

"When this is all over, I'll help you find them, Beru," I said.

Behind me, a loud burp interrupted our moment together. Thinking it was Ruta or maybe even Zeid, I turned around ready to give the offending person a look of disdain.

Instead, I found myself staring at five Ginete. Perhaps the five who set up the Remembering Ceremony, but these dwarf-like people all looked the same to me, so I wasn't sure. Besides, those huge golden eyes still scared the pants off me.

Where had they come from? Why were they here? Did I need another ceremony? All those questions flashed through my head before Beru left my side and flung herself into one of those dwarf's arms.

"Pita, I am so happy to see you and your brothers," she said.

After that, I had no idea what was said. It was a series of grunts, maybe burbs, whistles, and sighs that must have been language because the five of them seemed to be carrying on a conversation that they all understood. After a few more smiles and hugs, Beru must have remembered that I was there.

"You remember Pita and his brothers, don't you, Hannah?"

"Yes, of course," I said, faking it.

"Pita says my parents are safe in a village further east."

"That's fantastic, Beru. But why are Pita and his brothers here and how did they get here?"

"What they have to say is probably best said to the team all at once," Beru said, neatly avoiding answering how they got there. "That way there is no confusion, and we can all decide together what to do."

"About what?" I stupidly asked. Of course, I knew what it was about, didn't I? It's just that for a brief moment I had enjoyed the illusion of safety in a quaint town. I wanted to stay and explore, meet more of the people, maybe even learn about gardening. But I was sure that what Pita was there to tell us would mean something terrible was happening.

Lightning bolts were great and all that, but I would need more than that to fight off screaming blobs of green and a big shattering machine made of metal. Actually, when I said it to myself like that, it didn't sound all that bad.

Until I heard what Pita had to say. Then I was terrified all over again.

Thirty-Two

We stayed one more night in Kinver and decided not to have the meeting with the Ginete until morning.

"The news can wait," Pita said, "but not long."

I think everyone just needed one night of sleep inside and a chance to get really clean before heading back out on the road.

In the morning we gathered in the mayor's office. Even though our dimensions seemed worlds apart in some ways, in others it was very similar. The mayor's office reminded me of the one I knew back in the Earth Realm.

The Mayor told us that there was a small police force in Kinver that never had to do anything other than find a child who might have wandered too far from home, or rescue a cat or two.

But there was a disturbing trend of small pranks. Mean ones that would never have happened before. He wanted to know if we thought that it was the result of Abbadon's movement further east.

Suzanne had joined us for our meeting with the Ginete, so she was the one that answered.

"Yes, it probably is. Even though you can't hear the Shrieks yet, those sound waves are traveling around the planet. Sound affects everyone, even the ones that you can't hear. It could easily be disturbing people enough to make them act out.

"Even more reason to stop them before they move any further east. That uprising among your people will only get worse even if they never find your village. It could cause everything we love in Erda to self-destruct.

"Which means that we have to eliminate every Shriek. The problem is, we don't know how Abbadon is making them."

"Making them?" I asked. "I hadn't thought about that. So you are saying the Shrieks are not living beings, they are machines that Abbadon made?"

"They are a weapon, or weapons, that somehow Abbadon has produced," Suzanne answered. "They are not born from anything natural, they are human-made, or in this case, Abbadon made. But if he made them we can unmake them.

"There are a few problems with that, as you know. They are a sound weapon. As a weapon, they disable anything within the range of the sound that they make. It rarely kills, but it doesn't have to because Shatterskin comes right behind them, and it does the killing."

"Does the shrieking disable everything?" I asked.

Pita stepped in. "There are very few reports of anyone surviving the dual attack of the Shrieks and Shatterskin. But we have heard that some insects manage to keep on moving during the sound attack. They would have to move quickly out of the danger zone before Shatterskin arrives, though, because everything dies when he shatters."

"Is he using sound too?" I asked.

"That is a great question, Hannah. Yes, he is—not the same as the Shrieks. His sound is different. It is not designed to stun, but to shatter.

"Think of the stories you've heard about singers shattering

mirrors and glass on their high notes. It's akin to that."

"And do you know how Abbadon made Shatterskin, or what he runs on? Where's the energy that keeps him going?"

Zeid looked at me approvingly, and in spite of myself, I felt a tinge of satisfaction that I had pleased him.

"Now you are asking the right questions, Hannah," Suzanne said. "No, we don't know how Abbadon made Shatterskin, but we have an idea about how he is powering him. We have noticed that there is a brief cycle of time when Shatterskin is shut down, or off.

"A group of Shrieks arrive carrying something and swarm over him. When they withdraw, they are carrying something away. We are making a pretty valid assumption that it is some kind of battery. They are bringing it from the west and taking it back that way, so we think that Abbadon keeps on sending out fresh ones every few days.

"If we could block that supply line, even for a short time, we might be able to destroy Shatterskin as he runs out of juice. At least we could determine what kind of metal he is made from and from there determine how to stop him."

I turned to Pita and asked. "You said you have news for us?"

"Yes, I have good news and bad news. They are the same. Depends on which way you want me to tell it."

Ruta made a sound clearly indicating that Pita should just get on with it.

"The Riff has moved closer."

Inside my coat pocket, the Priscillas shivered. Everyone else just looked stunned. We all knew what it meant. We would get there sooner, but the Shrieks and Shatterskin were closer to towns and villages.

"They have destroyed thousands of acres of the country in just the last few weeks. At least one town that we know of was swallowed up. People don't escape. They can't move once that sound begins. If we could stop the sound, then they have a chance. Shatterskin moves slowly. He doesn't have to move quickly when there is no resistance."

Suzanne stood. "I have a piece of news that might be helpful. Dragons and our bird cousins have discovered something interesting. There are parts of the country that the Shrieks go around, and then of course so does Shatterskin.

"We don't know why. Nor do we know why they allow whatever was living there to continue. Perhaps because as those areas are surrounded by dead country, sooner or later the beings will starve anyway, and they don't want to waste time and energy on them."

"Or," Zeid broke in, "He has another weapon to take care of them."

Suzanne nodded. "Very possible. Perhaps that weapon comes after he has destroyed more of our land."

"What kind of country do they go around?" I asked.

"Swamps and salt flats."

"Must mean something," I mumbled.

"Yes, but what. Perhaps we can figure it out as we move out."

We all stood, ready to go. Niko thanked the Mayor of Kinver for his hospitality one more time.

The Mayor had turned an unflattering shade of green while we talked. Perhaps the reality of what Beru and Ruta had tried to tell him was becoming real to him. In any case, he managed to gather himself up enough to turn to Ruta and Beru to thank them for what they were doing.

"I pray that you find your parents, Beru," he said.

Beru, true to form, was gracious in her reply of thanks.

After Ruta and Beru left the room, I turned to Zeid and asked, "What about Ruta's parents? How come no one talks about them?"

"First, this isn't his village. Second, he knows what happened to his parents. It was their village that your mother was visiting when the Shrieks and Shatterskin destroyed it. It's why he is here. It's why he will give his life for yours as your mother tried to do for his family."

I was getting angrier every day. It was beginning to feel like it was a good thing. No more sweet Hannah. Princess Kara Beth was on the move.

I might not remember my mother, but I promised her that I would destroy the machines that killed her.

Thirty-Three

In the end, five men from the village came with us. I watched with a feeling of dread as they said goodbye to their families. One of the men was the father of the little girl I had noticed. I wanted to tell him to stay and take care of her, but I didn't.

It wasn't my choice. Each man had to do what he thought was the best thing for his family, but it still broke my heart watching them walk away from the ones that loved them. I would do everything I knew how to do to return them safe and sound.

Just before we left town, the little girl slipped up beside me, whispered that her name was Liza, put something in my hand, and then scampered away. I looked in my hand. Liza had given me her necklace. I had seen it on her—a small star sparkling in the sun. Now it was in my hand. When I started to go after her and give it back, Beru stopped me.

"This is Liza's way of keeping you safe, Hannah. Let it be."

I started to protest, but her father caught my eye and nodded. He knew. He wanted me to wear it too. Beru fastened it around my neck, and I hid it beneath my tunic. It was our secret. That tiny star was going to bring them all back. I swore it to myself.

We didn't march out of town down the road all together as I had envisioned. Suzanne returned to dragon form right in front of the villagers, and no one blinked an eye, reminding me that the people of Erda knew about magic. She headed into the woods where I knew she was scouting for the safest path to the Riff. Where the Ginete went, I had no idea. But Zeid assured me that they were traveling with us.

Cahir was waiting for me when we stepped back into the woods, and everyone gave me time to hug him and hide in his fur the tears that were always underneath the surface with me. The Priscillas had discovered that Cahir would sometimes let them hide in his coat, so they hopped out of my pocket and on to him. I couldn't blame them. Riding through the woods with a wolf sounded like freedom to me too.

Before moving on, I wanted to meet the five men that had chosen to come with us. The little girl's father's name was James, and his brother John had come too. They had left the third brother in the village to watch over their families and to care for the shop that their family owned in town. The last three were Kit, Mark, and Thomas, all farmers.

As they said their names, I thanked them for coming with us. I was afraid for them. They were weaponless, or so I thought. Then I remembered the day I had come to the Castle and all the people who had been there. Some were happy to see me, some were not, but they all had weapons.

The five men started laughing. They had caught what I was thinking? Ziffer, I needed to be careful. Now everyone could hear me. James answered for them, speaking out loud.

"No, we can't hear your thoughts. Your face gave you away. Besides, if I were you looking at us, I would wonder how we could be helpful without weapons. But we do have them. Each one of us has a skill that you might need.

"And if you are looking for a physical weapon, we have them too."

James nodded at the four other men, and all five had a weapon in their hand, either a staff, a sword, or a knife. When I looked again, they were gone.

"We don't need to display these. Weapons come when we need them. As far as hearing your thoughts, no we wouldn't do that, but we're tuned into the common channel that Professor Link set up for your team before you left the castle."

Once again I was caught flat-footed. "Professor Link? Is he monitoring the channel?" I asked.

"That he is," Niko said. "You don't think we would be heading out here without his support, do you? Think of him like you would a computer hacker back in Earth. You need something, he can tell you about it. Right now he is working on the ideas we learned yesterday from the Ginete."

"Like the insects escaping and the land the Shrieks and Shatterskin avoid?"

"Like that," Niko answered. "Now we need to get moving."

I grabbed his arm but removed my hand immediately when Niko scowled at me. What was I thinking? He could have probably chopped my hand off with a look.

"Sorry," I said. When I got another look both from Niko and Aki I stopped myself from descending into my sorry state and added, "Just one more thing. Can I talk to Professor Link, too."

"Of course," Niko said.

Great, I thought. But how?

The five men behind me laughed, and I did my best not to turn around and snap at them. Tears, anger, irritation, you never knew what you were going to get with me. I never knew what I was going to get with me.

Zeid smiled at me, and I felt better. "Let's go, Hannah. Link says he'll pop in later and talk to you if you haven't figured it out before then."

Nodding my thanks, I turned to follow Ruta into the woods. The men from the village fanned out, and I lost sight of them. Everyone in Erda was much more than they appeared on the surface. No, not everyone, everything.

As we walked, I thought about that. It was like there was another view of everything. In Earth, we had our five senses, and some people used other senses, like intuition, or paranormal abilities, to see what others couldn't see, but was there anyway.

In Erda there appeared to be even more than that. Instead of being a 3D world, perhaps it was a 4D world. I thought about Liza and the world she lived in and something clicked in my brain, and my eyes did something funny, and all of a sudden the entire world around me looked different.

It was like those magical pictures back home. Hidden within the pictures was a whole other picture which could only be seen when the eyes focused a different way.

"Holy, ziffer!" I yelled and stumbled forward and once again, fell flat on my face, just barely breaking my fall before my nose hit the ground. When I looked up again, everything was normal, or perhaps it was that I was blind once again.

Did I see what I thought I saw—or was it all illusion?

Thirty-Four

Zeid reached down and pulled me up trying hard not to laugh. I wasn't ready to tell him what I saw. I didn't know if it was something wrong with my brain, or if it was something everyone else saw all the time. Either way, I wanted to practice doing it on my own before I said anything to anyone.

"Still feeling clumsy I see," Zeid said. In that he was right, I was feeling clumsy and awkward, so I let it lie, for the moment. Instead, I changed the subject.

"What are our plans when we get to the Riff, Zeid," I asked. "We keep moving towards it, but I haven't heard anything about what we are going to do once we get there. And since it is moving closer to us every day, shouldn't we be preparing?"

"We have one more stop at a village. The people there have been working on ideas that we can use because, as you said, brute force is not going to win this battle. The Shrieks' sounds will incapacitate us before we can do anything to them. That's where the Ginete come in to play."

"The Ginete? You mean Pita and his brothers?"

"The same. We are stopping at their village tonight. They've gone ahead to make preparations."

My curiosity was peaked. A Ginete village. In my mind's

eye, I had it pictured as a quaint town peopled by little Ginete. I imagined their children as adorable miniatures of their parents making them look like cousins of ET. So later that day when Niko held up his hand for us to stop and Zeid whispered that we were there, I was perplexed.

We were standing in the middle of the forest. It looked like every other part of the woods with trees, ferns, and moss. No village. I was just ready to mouth off at Zeid when a Ginete I thought was Pita popped up five feet in front of me.

"What? Where did you come from?" I asked.

Pita pointed to the ground.

"You came from the ground? That's impossible!" I said.

Pita just pointed at the ground again, and I swear he smirked at me. I heard Ruta laugh his frog croaking laugh. Even the Priscillas who had positioned themselves on my shoulder were giggling. By now, everyone had gathered around me. I could see Cahir sitting outside the group. If wolves could laugh, I think he was.

"Stop kidding around you guys. This isn't funny," I shouted at everyone. By then the five men from Kinver had joined the group and were laughing. Only James kept his face impassive, but I knew he was trying hard not to laugh.

I looked back at Pita, and he was gone. I stamped my foot. This was stupid. I knew I looked ridiculous stamping my foot in anger, but I couldn't help it. Everyone laughed even harder. I got even angrier. I looked back, and Pita was there.

My head felt as if it was going to explode. Everyone was making fun of me. I was literally going crazy. I looked back at James to try to gain some stability, and he touched his throat. What was he trying to tell me? Was he trying to remind me about his daughter, Liza? Did I have time for this?

James tilted his head and touched his throat again. My star.

He was pointing to the star that his daughter had given me. I reached up and touched it, and then it happened again.

My focus went wonky, and I saw the world differently. The forest contained much more than I thought was possible. Instead of being a sea of various shades of green and brown with flashes of color as the birds flitted from tree to tree, the whole forest was a riot of colors in all shades and tones. It could have been too much, but it wasn't. It was beautiful, like a canvas painted by a master artist.

It was not only the color that made it different. There were plants I had never seen before growing between the trees, and on the trees. Birds I didn't know were perched on limbs of trees that spread out underneath the canopy. I couldn't even see what tree the limbs belonged to. Everything was intertwined, and yet there was space between them, so it felt open and free.

Looking up, I saw the same sky I had seen before, but instead of one shade of blue, it was marbled blue. The light from the sun streaked through the forest as it usually did, but these streaks sparkled. The air was filled with fragrances I recognized and those I didn't. I thought I could even hear the sounds of the insects as they moved on the forest floor and through the trees.

Everyone around me seemed both more substantial and less at the same time. Everyone had stopped laughing. They were waiting as if they knew what was happening.

I heard a voice in my head and realized that it was Professor Link.

"While your mind is open, remember what this feels like. Remember that most of the time you are not seeing everything that there is to see, or feel, or smell. There is much more to the universe around you than your mind can hold most of the time.

"You used the star Liza gave you to get here, but you won't always need it. When this vision fades, you will still see more than you saw before, and yes, now your channel to me has been turned on."

Before I had time to answer Link, he was gone, but I heard Zeid say, "Now look at Pita."

Yes, he was there again, and still pointing down, but this time I could see that he was standing on a circle on the ground, and as I watched, it whooshed down, and he was gone. The earth closed behind him.

As I looked around, everything faded back to the world as I knew it, except I could feel my channel to Link in my mind, and I could see a small blue light on the ground where the circle had been. As I watched, Pita rose again. This time he said, "Welcome, Hannah, to our village."

Within seconds I felt the ground move beneath my feet.

I screamed.

Thirty-Five

Imagine Santa's workshop at the North Pole. You know, all those cute little elves running around in a bright Disneyland space. Maybe some jolly dwarf singing dwarf songs.

Once I realized that I was still alive after descending at a breakneck speed down into the ground and before I managed to open my eyes, I had a brief flash thinking that was the kind of scene I would see.

So wrong. Instead, every member of our team was standing inside a vast room. Pita and his four brothers were there, and if I interpreted their facial expressions correctly, they were smiling.

But it wasn't a Disneyland scene at all. The room was empty, and to me, a little too warm. As if he could read my mind, Pita said, "It's always about this temperature, which is what makes living underground so perfect."

"That and other things," grunted one of the brothers. Pita nodded his approval.

"We have food prepared for you, and after that, we can look over the equipment that you ordered,' Pita said to Niko, who answered, "Lead on, Pita. We are looking forward to meeting your brethren and sharing the table with them."

I barely registered that they were talking because I was

busy taking in the details of where we were. Although we were underground, the air was fresh. The light seemed to be coming from the walls, much like it did in the castle. This time though, the walls were made of what looked like intertwined branches, or since we were underground, perhaps they were roots.

One of Pita's brothers hung back and walked with me. He asked me if I would like him to explain what I was seeing. "Yes, but I don't know your name.

"Tita," he replied.

"Pita and Tita?"

"Pita, Tita, Bita, Lita, and Sam," he answered.

I burst out laughing, and he joined along holding his ears as he did so. I wasn't sure if it was because he laughed so rarely he didn't know where to put his hands, or if that was a standard way for a Ginete to laugh, since I had never seen one of them laugh that hard before.

Tita's big golden eyes were sparkling when we both stopped laughing.

"I know. I think our mother ran out of things that rhymed with Pita by the time Sam arrived. Lita doesn't like his name too much. Says it sounds like a girl's name. But no one crosses our mom."

"Well, I am looking forward to meeting such a lovely woman, Tita," I said. "And yes, please explain what I am looking at."

By then we were deep into a large tunnel. I had no sense of direction, but Tita said we were heading northwest.

"We have a network of tunnels and rooms all over the Kingdom. Your Kingdom, Princess," Tita said bowing a bit. When I shook my head at the title, he countered, "It's important that you take back this role. Our people, all the people of the Kingdom of Zerenity, need to know that you are here for them.

Not the little girl from the Earth dimension, but the woman who has returned to Erda."

I knew that Tita was right. But I wasn't ready to say it out loud to anyone, yet. Besides, it was the first time I had heard that "my" kingdom had a name. Zerenity sounded like serenity with a z, so I assumed that they meant about the same thing. There were many questions that needed answering, but this was not the time. So I diverted the attention back to his home.

"How are these tunnels made? Do you build them, and how do these walls stay up like this?"

"No, our cousins build them. And the trees fortify them. Without trees, none of this would exist, and I don't mean just our home.

"All of life on the planet would not exist without trees, and that's what makes Abbadon so incredibly dangerous. It's why we call him the Evil One. The Destroyer. His plan will destroy every tree on the planet. After that, there is only death."

"Well, then, how does he expect to live?"

Tita gave me a look of such profound sorrow I felt the pain of it run the entire length of my body. There was a story here that they had not yet told me. I couldn't imagine what could be worse than what I had already heard, but then, imagining ultimate Evil had never been something I wanted to do.

I put my hand on Tita's arm. "I'm sorry, Tita, I understand if you don't want to talk about this now. I'm sure I will learn when it is the right time to know."

Tita nodded at me gratefully, and we continued our walk down the tunnel together. I could see that it opened into another room, and could hear the current of lively chatter and laughter coming from it.

"Your cousins?" I asked. "Your cousins built the tunnels? Who are your cousins?"

Tita laughed again. "We lovingly call them 'Whistle Pigs.' You call them groundhogs."

"Groundhogs are your cousins?" I asked in amazement. I knew groundhogs. They dug holes in the ground and pulled plants into them. They were the bane of farmers everywhere. "Groundhogs did all of this?"

"Well, okay, not groundhogs as you know them. These are groundhogs!" Tita said pulling me through the door and opening his arms to take in the scene.

I recognized my team and the Ginete, but what were those huge hairy things that looked like bears?

"Those are our Whistle Pigs, Hannah. The best friend the people of Erda have ever had. And one of the best lines of defense you will have in your fight against the Shrieks."

I stood there with my mouth hanging open. Not attractive. But real. I hoped Tita was right because if those groundhogs, Whistle Pigs, were not on our side, we were in serious trouble.

One broke free of the group he had been talking with and ambled over to where Tita stood with me grinning from ear to ear.

"Teddy," he said, "This is Princess Kara Beth."

I was too shocked to correct him. In fact, I realized I better step up into the Princess role if I ever expected to have a stand with this bear of a being. "Seriously, your name is Teddy? Like a Teddy bear?"

"Just like that, Miss Princess," Zeid joked in my head.

I couldn't afford to turn and give him a dirty look. What would Teddy do?

Instead, I bowed my head and stuck out my hand. Teddy took it between his massive paws and said, "At your service."

Inwardly I sighed in relief. I had passed some first test. I was sure that there were more.

Thirty-Six

That dinner was the rowdiest dinner I had ever attended. Turns out the combination of Whistle Pigs and Ginete is loud. Add some kind of strong drink, that Zeid warned me not to taste, and the effect is multiplied. Within an hour, Teddy and Pita were dancing on tables together singing louder than I ever thought possible.

All of Pita's brothers eventually joined in, and when two more Whistle Pigs ambled into the room looking as if they just finished digging another tunnel, they incited even more laughter and dancing. The room felt as if it was vibrating from floor to ceiling. I could barely eat for the noise. But what I had was delicious.

The tables around the room were filled with food. At first, I thought it was because it was easier to have us serve ourselves, which might have been true, but then I realized it was probably to leave the tables in the center of the room free for pounding hands and dancing feet.

I caught sight of some Ginete that I didn't know constantly replenishing the supply of food and drink. They would quickly glance around the room before they left, and if I caught their eye, they would bow and walk backward until they were out of sight. I made a mental note to stop that kind of practice if I ever got the chance to have things my way.

At the first sight of Teddy, the Priscillas had hidden in my pocket, and as the noise worsened, they abandoned me altogether, saying they were off to explore, and would be back soon. I wished that I could go with them, but I couldn't escape.

Every ten minutes or so, someone would hold up their glass and toast, to "Princess Kara Beth," or "to the Kingdom of Zerenity. May it endure." Then all heads would swivel my way, and I would hold my glass of water and toast with them.

I was beyond grateful that Zeid stayed by my side, poking me if my attention wandered, and keeping the worst of the exuberant behavior at least a few feet away from me. Once I almost got dragged up to a table to dance, but a swift glance from Niko, who magically appeared beside me, stopped any further shenanigans of that kind.

Not long after that—either Niko's presence, or the food, or the drink got to them—the Ginete and Whistle Pigs started slowing down. Some even put their heads on a table and fell asleep.

"We can go now," Suzanne said, reaching for my hand. Suzanne still looked perky and fresh, whereas I felt as if someone had been hitting me over the head with a hammer. I was torn between admiring the commitment to entertaining themselves in spite of the danger we were facing, and wondering why they would do such a thing knowing what we had to do.

Either way, I was exhausted and happy to follow Suzanne if she would just get me away from the craziness. She led me down another tunnel to a small cozy room with the most comfortable bed I had ever seen.

The room was just big enough for a bed and a table beside it. Within seconds I was under the covers still wearing all my clothes. Just before falling asleep I wondered if the next day would bring as many revelations.

"Different ones," Suzanne whispered.

****

The only way I could tell it was morning was that my cozy little bedroom was filled with light. The bed and the room felt so pleasant, part of me wanted to stay underground with the Ginete forever.

As I lay in bed wishing I never had to get up, the Priscillas came fluttering into the room looking a little weary. I had forgotten that they had left during the party. I wondered what they had been doing that made them look so tired.

"Up, up, Hannah," Pris said. "Zeid said you have to be ready for the strategy meeting in an hour. We found you a shower."

"And your clothes are clean too," La piped in. "We took them down to the laundry last night."

"Are you trying to tell me I stink?" I laughed.

When the three of them exchanged looks, I knew. Of course, they were always riding with me. Even Cahir's fur probably smelled better than me after a while.

It was only then that I realized that someone had undressed me in order to clean my clothes. I was afraid to ask who that was. Cil pointed to a robe on the bed, and I headed off to the showers with the Priscillas leading the way.

An hour later I was seated in what could have been a conference room anywhere in Earth, except there were no windows. And of course, there were beings there having coffee together that I would never have seen anywhere at any table at home.

Teddy was at the head of the table. His fur was slightly wet, so I assumed that he too had taken a shower. Actually, everyone in the room looked fresh and alert. Each of us had a mug of something in front of us. Mine was coffee, made just the way that I like it.

After all the pleasantries were exchanged, Teddy cleared his throat and began. He told us that the Ginete and the Whistle Pigs had been working on something that would protect people from the Shrieks, the theory being that if we were not affected by them, we could kill them, and half the battle would be won.

Staying underground was one way to be protected. The earth and the tree roots blocked most of the sound, and almost no one was bothered by any residual sounds that might seep through.

But being underground did not stop Shatterskin. He shattered underground Ginete villages as if they were made of glass.

The Whistle Pigs, who usually lived even further underground than the Ginete, would sometimes escape the Shattering. But when they came out into the woods after Shatterskin had gone by, there was nothing left to eat. Starvation killed many of them.

"Let me take you to what we have made for you," Teddy said, getting up from the table.

He led us across the hall and opened the door. At first there appeared to be nothing there except for a long table across the back of the room, and workbenches lining the sides.

"O...kay," I said.

Teddy laughed, a big gruff contagious "haha." I almost joined in, not even understanding the joke, but managed to contain myself just in time.

That made Teddy laugh even harder, until finally, he said, "Okay. Show yourselves."

Within a split second the room was filled with Ginete and

Whistle Pigs. A split second later they were gone again. And then back. That time they stayed and I could see they all had something attached to their arms.

"Wow," Niko said and reached over and shook Teddy's massive paw. "You guys did it!"

Thirty-Seven

"There's more, of course. These are only one line of defense and also part of your offense," Teddy said.

"Sorry for being dense, but what is it?" I asked.

Teddy ambled to a workbench and brought back what looked like a thin slice of metal with a strap on the back. I recognized the shape when he held it that way.

"It's a shield. Okay." I said.

Teddy helped me fit it onto my arm. I was delighted how light it was. Even I could lift it. Wow, a shield just for me. I was beginning to feel like a warrior princess.

The Ginete got a shield off the workbench for everyone and fit them onto their arms. Each shield was a different size depending on the person. Even Beru and Ruta had a shield. The Priscillas looked like they were pouting that they didn't have one, but I assured them that they could stay behind mine. I tried not to laugh at the thought of little fairy shields. I didn't want to insult them.

It was only after everyone had their shield on, that I fully realized that when someone had the shield in front of them, they disappeared.

"Holy ziffer," I shouted. "This is cool! But how does this help us with the Shrieks? Don't they shriek all the time whether they see people or not? Why would it help to be invisible?"

"You're right," Niko said. "They constantly shriek as they move. Moving and shrieking seem to be the only skills that they have. Even when they rest, if the Shrieks sense movement they will shriek. We're not even sure if they are resting, or waiting for orders. I don't think they have an off button.

"Besides making you invisible, these shields are made to block sound. Blocking light and sound go together enough to make this work. However, they will only block sound long enough to keep you functioning for a few more seconds. It's what the shields do after that that makes them effective."

Niko gestured at Teddy to take over.

"These shields not only make you invisible and block the first burst of sound, but most importantly they reflect sound. But not all the time. You need to turn the switch on to make that part work. Find it now, but do not for any reason turn it on."

Once we all found the switch which was easily reached with the hand holding the shield, Teddy continued. "This is why you need those extra few seconds of consciousness. You need to get to that switch."

"Why not leave it always on?" I asked. Always the girl with questions.

"It uses the properties of a mirror," Teddy replied.

Teddy paused and waited for me to get it. In all the time I had been in Erda I had never seen a mirror. I remembered that Beru had told me they believed that Abbadon could use a mirror to see what was on the other side.

"So that means it will be possible for Abbadon to see us as we reflect the sound and send it back to the Shrieks?"

"Exactly. So when you turn the shield on you will have to

be quick. You will have to aim the shield precisely so that you reflect all the sound to the Shrieks and not somewhere else. We think that when we direct their shrieks back to them, they will become immobilized."

"You think?" I asked, feeling the dread deep into my stomach.

"We think. I wish we could more sure, but we obviously didn't have any Shrieks to practice on. However, based on our sound studies and the reports we have received from our dragon and bird friends about how the Shrieks move, we have concluded that their own sounds can hurt them."

Looking around the room, Teddy continued. "We know we aren't giving you an absolute, but we believe that this is the right conclusion as to why the Shrieks move in a straight line, side by side, through the forest, when scattering unevenly would be more effective. Think about how a group of people move when they are searching for something. A straight line with very little space between them, that's what they look like.

"We reason that they don't want the sounds to hit each other. Traveling in a straight line keeps them out of the range of the sound that is being projected forward. The shrieking moves as a cone directly in front of each Shriek. Afterward, the shrieking disperses and is not as deadly.

"Not only do the Shrieks travel in a straight line, but they also move as one when they turn. If as they travel through the land something survives behind them, they all stop, swivel, shriek, and after that being is stunned or dead they swivel back and move on."

All of us nodded. What Teddy said made sense.

"But will it be enough?" Aki asked what all of us were wondering.

"Well, we don't see why not. We have made the mirror ultra-reflective by magnifying it at five hundred times."

"Doesn't that mean there is a chance that if the Shrieks have missed someone behind them, that we might be the ones that stun or kill them?" I asked.

"Yes. There is that chance. So don't turn your shields on unless they are pointed directly at a Shriek, and there is no one behind them. It's dangerous, but we believe that with it you will stun, or perhaps kill every Shriek you use it on."

"What if it doesn't kill them, just stuns them, and after a time they turn back on and start shrieking?" I asked.

"You're right, little Princess," Teddy said. I was beginning to like hearing Teddy say my name. In spite of the fact he was describing the horrific danger we were walking into, he looked so cuddly. Except when he smiled. Whoa, those teeth.

"We have plans for killing. You stun them first. Then you can kill them. Shatterskin will still be doing his thing, but once we get rid of his minions, we have a chance against him. It may be as simple as killing the Shrieks that bring him the power, waiting until he runs out of power, and attacking him then."

"Assuming that's how he operates," James said.

"And assuming he's killable," his brother John added.

"Yes, assuming all that," Niko said.

"You know how in Earth they say it takes a village to raise a child, Hannah?" Suzanne asked.

I nodded, wondering where she was going with this analogy.

"Well, that's true. It does. It will also take a community to kill the Shrieks and Shatterskin. It's the one weapon we have that we know Abbadon does not have. He has nothing but himself. We have all of us, and those that wait for us topside."

"Oh, that reminds me," Teddy said. "You have another weapon here. Us. The Whistle Pig community will be right beneath your feet monitoring what's happening. If we have to, we'll drop you into one of our tunnels."

"That puts you at risk too, though doesn't it, Teddy? If we fail, Shatterskin will kill all of you."

"If you fail, we are all dead anyway," Pita said.

Nothing like doomsday words to cheer a girl up.

Thirty-Eight

The friendship bracelet that Johnny had given me before I left Earth was still on my arm as I held the shield in front of me. I loved how the bracelet helped me discern my right hand from my left hand. I often got confused which hand I was using when training with Niko and Zeid. I kept the bracelet on my left arm to remind me that was my left hand, and it reminded me of what I had left behind.

I also had the bracelet that Professor Link had given me. Even though it had felt familiar when I put it on my arm, I still didn't know why I had it. Although it too was on my left arm, it wasn't a reminder of what I had left behind, but of what I couldn't remember.

Niko had us all practicing with our shields in the transport room. It was perfect for practicing. There was nothing in the space except for us and targets on the walls that the Ginete had put up. There was nothing to trip over except our own feet. Well, that was me, not necessarily anyone else.

Although the shields were lightweight, it still felt awkward swinging it around and making sure we aimed it correctly. We weren't practicing with the real shields. Not only wasn't there any shrieking to reflect, but we also couldn't afford to turn on the mirrors and show Abbadon where we were. I wondered how Teddy and his crew had managed to make the shield without alerting Abbadon.

"Very carefully, Miss Kara," Teddy said coming up beside me. He changed what he called me every time we saw each other. I wondered if it was his personality that loved the creativity of finding new names for me. It seemed reasonable considering how creative he and his team would have to be to build the shields.

The shields Teddy and his crew had provided for our practice shot out paintballs so we could see where we had aimed. At first, we were terrible. Switch on, shoot. Switch off, turn. And repeat constantly. It was hard to do, especially considering how fast we had to move.

We had live "targets" to practice with, too—willing Ginete dressed in green suits simulated attacking us. If what we were doing wasn't so dangerous, I would have laughed at the sight.

The goal was to cover those green suits with paint. But at first, we covered each other, which scared the ziffer out of me. We would be killing ourselves while fighting the Shrieks.

After an hour of mock fighting, we took a break. The Ginete changed suits and washed off the walls. They assured us that the trees weren't hurt, the paint was vegetable based and would soak through the ground without harm to anyone.

Each of us had a different color paint shooting from our shields. Not surprisingly, Niko's red was rarely seen other than on a green suit, but my yellow was everywhere. I was more dangerous with my shield than the Shrieks.

During the next hour, we all got a little better, so someone turned on some loud shrieking kind of music. After that, we all got worse again. And we didn't improve much over that next hour.

It was more than embarrassing to see yellow paint on everyone and everything except for on the green-suited Ginete.

When we broke for lunch, I went to speak to Niko. "I can't do this Niko. I'll kill everyone. Give me something else to do."

"No."

"No? Aren't you afraid of what I might do?" I asked.

"Absolutely terrified, Hannah. But you have to lead your people. If you don't, there won't be a Kingdom to rule. It will divide into factions. Communities that have existed for thousands of years will crumble because their faith will have crumbled first.

"So learn to control yourself first, and then your shield, because that's the only way we will defeat Abbadon. The Shrieks are only his first line of attack. Get through them, and then there is Shatterskin.

"And after that … well, let's take one at a time shall we."

I hung my head in shame and terror. I would kill them all before Shatterskin even arrived.

"Or not," Pris said in my ear. Niko couldn't hear her, but he saw something gather itself inside of me. That little fire I had found had not gone out, and Pris's words made me think that I could build it and use it. After all, where did that bolt of lightning come from anyway?

"Where did it come from, Hannah?" Niko asked. "Find the source. Let it direct you. Get rid of the ideas about yourself that you brought here. The past may teach you something, but that's all its good for. It's not a place to hide, or wallow."

I stared at Niko hoping that his words would stoke the fire, and as I turned to go, he said, "Hannah, I believe in you."

Everyone believed in me. If I couldn't believe in myself, the least I could do was trust in the people that cared about me.

I lifted my shield, switched it on, and shot the target on the wall, dead on. Switch on, switch off, shoot. A clean shot every time.

After lunch with the room swarming with green-suited Ginete, and vibrating with the loudest noise I had ever heard, I managed to hit only green suits most of the time.

Zeid put his arm around my shoulder and pulled me close. His purple paintballs had hit every target. Only one had missed. We both knew that one was one too many, but it was a thousand times better than when we had begun that morning.

"Great job, Hannah Banana," He said.

"Hannah Banana?"

"Teddy is not the only one who can make up interesting names," Zeid laughed. Getting serious he said, "We both need more practice, but everyone else seems to be doing well."

"I think we are the only ones who aren't one-hundred percent, Zeid. But I know you will be, and I will be too. Even if I can't shoot fireballs out of my hands all the time, at least I can get good at aim, switch, shoot, switch." I said.

Zeid was almost at the tunnel leading to dinner when he turned, "Why can't you Hannah? Why can't you access the talents you already possess all the time? Lightning bolts are a small version of what you can do. What are you afraid of? And don't tell me that it's the Shrieks, Shatterskin, or Abbadon. This is something personal.

"Maybe it's time for you to visit the Oracle and get a little mental adjustment. Or maybe a big one."

"What Oracle? Will that help? Because if the answer is yes, can you take me there?"

"I'll clear it with Niko and Aki. If they say yes I'll take you there myself after dinner."

Zeid waited for a beat and then said, "Come on you lazy butt. I'll race you to dinner."

Without waiting for my consent, he started down the hall towards the dining room. No way was I going to let him beat me, even if he did have an unfair head start.

Thirty-Nine

Niko and Aki gave Zeid permission to take me to the Oracle, but only after I spent another hour shooting targets with the music at full blast, and with Zeid running around distracting me. If I could shoot accurately for fifteen minutes, I had the rest of the night off. What we did with the time was up to us.

But I saw Niko's face when Zeid asked him. I wondered if it wasn't all a setup.

Once again, the Priscillas went somewhere without telling me where they were going. They didn't belong to me, but it worried me a bit that they were off doing who knows what and coming back looking bedraggled. It was one of those things that I couldn't control though.

It took me two hours of practice before I got fifteen minutes of entirely accurate shooting. I was exhausted. Everything ached. "Forget the Oracle," I said. "I need sleep."

"Not going to happen, Hannah," Zeid said. The appointment has been made. You are expected."

It was useless to argue. We stopped at the workroom to hang up our shields. Aki was waiting for us. She smiled at Zeid and said, "I'll take it from here, Zeid." When he didn't immediately move, she added, "I promise, I'll take good care of her."

"This was planned all along, wasn't it?" I asked Aki as soon as Zeid was out of sight. "Like getting me so tired I can barely walk. Having Zeid set it up. All planned."

"Life is all planned, Hannah. What we do with it is what changes it."

"Multiple outcomes?"

"All stories, Hannah. Which one do you choose to live?"

"What am I in this one, Aki?"

"Ah. That's the question, isn't it? Are you the poor maiden, or are you the princess who saves them all. Or maybe something in between."

"It can't be that simple, Aki," I said.

"But that's not all that simple, is it? If all of this is a story, how in depth is the story? Does it change within each dimension? Are you one thing here, and one thing there? If you make a wrong choice, does it ruin everything? These are very complicated questions," Aki said.

"If you want to know what choices you have made so far, look at your life. Life is a mirror. It reflects back to us what we believe, what we think we deserve, and how we feel about other creatures. Most people are afraid to look in that mirror. Perhaps they fear that their personal version of the Evil One will be staring back at them. But without looking, we are prisoners of our beliefs."

By then we had reached a door at the end of the tunnel. It reminded me of a hobbit door. Round at the top, small enough I would have to duck to get through. A knocker with the face of a wolf hung on the door. All of a sudden, I missed Cahir. I hoped he was doing well up top.

"What am I going to learn here?" I asked Aki.

The look she gave me was the answer. I would learn what I

wanted to learn. As I knocked, I wondered what that was. One thing I knew for sure. I did not want to be the poor maiden in the story.

****

The next morning I woke up again without my clothes on, a robe on the bed, and wondered if I had better find out who was undressing me.

This time, instead of the Priscillas waiting for me to wake up, it was Aki. Normal people sleep in a bed or chair, right? Aki was sleeping in the air. I remembered how she would levitate into our yoga classes back in the castle and wondered if this was the same or if I couldn't see what was holding her up.

As my hand reached to the star around my neck, Aki opened her eyes and stared at me. For a second I felt as if I was being stared at by a snake. The moment passed, but the feeling continued as she uncurled herself and sat up.

"That star is not there for you just when you are curious, or bored. Use it cautiously. Practice getting there without touching it." Aki slipped off of something and levitated to the bed. Yes, something was holding her up as she slept, and yes she could still levitate.

"First thing in the morning you are lecturing me," I teased, and then realized my mistake. Aki scowled and said, "Breakfast in twenty. Be clean." And then she was gone.

I knew that look. I grabbed the robe, the clean clothes on my chair, and rushed down the hall to the shower. It would have been lovely to stand under water that I could get as hot as I wanted for a long time, but I knew that Aki was serious. Being late was not an option.

It wasn't until I began to put on my clothes that I

remembered. The door, the wolf knocker, ducking into a dark room…and then nothing. After that, I remembered nothing. At all. Not good.

Once I had my tunic on, the Priscillas showed up and arranged themselves on my shoulder and fell asleep. They looked like pretty pins resting there. I resisted the temptation to pull Pris's pigtails. Why were they so sleepy? Where were they going at night?

All these thoughts were going through my head as I ran through the halls to get to breakfast on time. Everyone was there, waiting for me. And someone else, Earl. Earl was sitting at the head of the table. No one was talking. Everyone was staring at me.

Earl. I hadn't seen him since the castle, and then only a few times. He had met me there when we came out of the woods and had dinner with us. After that, he had stopped by once or twice, but he never stayed to have dinner. And never to wear the look on his face that he had on then.

No one had food in front of them. I had a feeling that what Earl was going to say was going to kill my appetite too. I lowered myself in the one empty chair. The one directly opposite from Earl. Zounds, something was really wrong, and I prayed that it wasn't because of something that I had done, or not done.

It turned out that it was worse than I could have imagined. Our time was up. Our training was over. The Shrieks were only a day away. The Riff had come to us.

Forty

"What did you learn from the Oracle?" Zeid asked. Aki heard him ask and looked my way, so I answered them both.

"I have no ziffing idea. I can't remember a thing."

"Nothing?" Zeid asked, looking as puzzled as I felt. I wasn't surprised to see that Aki smiled and looked away. I had a feeling she had something to do with my memory loss, and perhaps my continual waking up in bed without clothes.

I was grateful for that part. Clean clothes every morning was a true luxury, and one that I didn't expect again for some time.

"Nothing."

"Well, do you feel different?" Zeid asked.

It was the right question to ask because I did. It was hard to put my finger on it, but perhaps my intention of not being the poor maiden in the story turned the tide.

"If you are asking if I feel any more magical than I did before, the answer is no. If you are asking if I feel better about myself, the answer is yes," I said.

We had packed our backpacks and were headed to the workroom to pick up our real shields. The shields that could kill the wrong people if not used correctly. The ones that the day before had terrified me. But not anymore. At least it wasn't the same. The terror was still there, but instead of feeling like a lid pressing down on me, it felt like a match. If lit it could start a fire. I was ready for it.

That was something I couldn't or wouldn't explain, so I answered Zeid with a grunt. He laughed and jogged over to where the rest of the team was waiting. Everyone was ready. Even the Priscillas looked more alert than they had the last few days. Perhaps the nap on my shoulder was enough for them.

Standing on the little blue circles that glowed in the practice space and waiting to be lifted to the surface made me think of Star Trek. "Beam me up, Scotty," I said, and everyone laughed.

A second later they were all gone, including the Priscillas who had attached themselves to Aki instead of me. Didn't occur to me how weird that was until that moment. I was still standing there by myself. "Sorry about that, Princess Kara Beth," Teddy said, coming over to where I stood.

"No nickname this time, Teddy?" I scoffed and then saw his face.

"What is it?"

"I had to give you this," Teddy said, holding up a little circle as small as a button. He placed it on my skin under the neck of my shirt on the left-hand side. The side with the two bracelets. My shield side. The pin was so light I wouldn't have known that it was there if he hadn't told me what he was doing.

"What is it?"

"A safety button. If something happens and you are trapped, press it, and you will be rescued."

"What will happen then? And why not give it to everyone?"

"Because it's you that has to survive."

We stared at each other for what felt like an eternity. It was my choice what to do with what Teddy had just said. Was it a curse, or was it a blessing that I would live even if my friends died?

Teddy pushed the answer to my question into my mind, where it would stay. "If you live, you have a chance to save them. If you die, they will die too."

"What will you do if I am trapped?"

"Best you don't know," Teddy said.

The next second I was above ground where the team was waiting for me. No one looked worried. Well, Zeid did. But everyone else was calm. Did they know what happened with Teddy and me, or was that just the way that they were?

Above ground I hadn't realized how much I had missed the sun, the air, the top part of the trees. It was glorious. I spun around, arms open, face to the sun. I wanted to remember how good this felt when we faced the Shrieks. They wanted to take away all this beauty from everyone.

Well, they probably didn't want anything. Shrieks were mindless robots doing the bidding of Abbadon. Someday, I didn't know how, or when, I will stop Abbadon. Kill him if I have to, I vowed to myself,

"That was different," Zeid said coming up beside me.

"What?"

"That feeling. The depth of it. It was scary. Maybe the Oracle did something after all."

"Perhaps," I acknowledged to Zeid. To myself it wasn't a perhaps, it was a certainty. I was ready for whatever magic I had to show itself.

"No matter what?" Link asked.

I had forgotten about Professor Link and his open channel.

"Have you been there all along?" I asked, a little pissed. No, a lot pissed. This was ridiculous. People always in my mind.

"Then shut it off, Hannah. You have the power to do so. On the other hand, do you have the time to reopen it in an emergency?"

I knew I didn't, so I sighed, and pushed the thought back to him. "Be polite, please. Don't snoop."

"As if! Never!" Link said, in a Valley girl voice.

We both laughed.

"What's so funny?" Zeid asked.

"Link, impersonating a Valley girl," I answered.

"Oh, yea. Link does that sometimes. Not just Valley girls, but characters throughout human history in Earth. Probably keeps his mind from freaking out with all that he has to do to keep us safe."

I nodded and pushed to Link, "Have I said thank you?"

A picture of a sad little puppy floated by in my head. I laughed again.

"Link?" Zeid asked.

I didn't have time to answer because Niko made a hand circle for all of us to gather close to him.

"Are you ready? All of you?" He asked glancing around the circle.

Zeid, Aki, Beru, Ruta, the five Ginete brothers, James and the four other men from Kinver all nodded grimly. The Priscillas had returned to me and tittered their answer of "yes."

Cahir was waiting in the woods. I could see him watching, wary. Suzanne had shapeshifted to Lady and was flying above us. A black, white, and red dragon. Guarding and protecting.

Niko stopped and rested his gaze on me. I answered with as much assurance as I could muster, "Ready."

With one last glance around to take in our surroundings, we once again followed Ruta through the woods.

"How far away is the Riff, Zeid?" I asked.

Zeid inclined his head to Niko, so I turned my gaze to him.

"It moves closer. A day or less."

"You know I never asked what the Riff looks like. How will I know that we are there?"

"Besides the green blobs screaming with their entire bodies? On one side will be life, on the other side will be death. There will be no mistaking it."

Forty-One

The morning walk was peaceful. Especially considering where we were going. Even though the practice time had been intense, a few days of a good night's sleep, clean clothes and bodies, had lifted everyone's spirits in spite of the danger that lay ahead.

The Priscillas seemed to have recovered from their nightly excursions and were flitting ahead of us on the trail. It was unusual. Since the ceremony, they had spent most of their time in my coat pocket or riding on my shoulder. I was a little hurt that they didn't appear to need me anymore. Yes, it was petty. Still, I sulked.

So when Pris came back and rested on my shoulder, I decided to be direct and ask her what was going on. Why weren't they riding with me? Where had they been every night?

What was I thinking? That I had a right to ask? Apparently not, because Pris got angry. Fast. I had forgotten how intense she could be. The first thing she did was fly to my face and beat her little fists on my forehead. "Ow, ow," I said trying to keep from hurting her as I attempted to brush her away, or hold her still.

It was interesting that in spite of my frantic efforts to get her to stop pounding on me, no one looked my way, or even showed a glimmer of interest. No one except Link who I could hear laughing in the background.

Ignoring him, I tried to tell Pris that I was sorry, not sure what I was sorry for, but her little fists were like tiny battering rams. Hearing the noise, Cil and La came flying out of the woods like tiny bees ready for a fight. I was in deep trouble.

Except they didn't attack me. Instead, Cil and La grabbed Pris and pulled her away and put her on my shoulder. They were careful not to put her close enough so she could pull my ear. Once Pris had settled down, La flew up into a tree and brought back what turned out to be a dab of honey on her fingertip which she rubbed on my red forehead. It immediately felt better.

"What did you say to her anyway?" Cil asked.

"I just asked where you all went at night and why you weren't riding with me as much anymore."

"Oh," La said."The Oracle didn't tell you?"

When I gave her a blank look, Cil added, "That explains it."

"Yep, it does," La agreed.

I was lying in a way because what the Oracle told me was starting to seep back into my mind. But something told me to keep quiet about it for now. Besides, I had asked Pris a perfectly reasonable question because I didn't know where they were going at night. As far as I knew, the Oracle had not told me that.

But I still didn't understand what made Pris so mad. "Is it a bad thing to wonder where you went at night? You know where I am all the time."

"True," Cil said. "We do. I suppose we trust that you will remember more about us soon. So, we might as well tell you, since you are a sister and all, what we have been up to."

A sister? Cil must have picked up that phrase from

somewhere, but I went with it.

Pris piped up, "If someone is going to tell her, it's going to be me."

She had just opened her mouth to tell me when we all heard it. A shriek. Not as loud as we had heard them before, but it was definitely a shriek. If we weren't sure what it was, it didn't take long to confirm our fears. Within seconds birds and animals started coming our way, fleeing as fast as they could from something behind them.

"That's our cue," Niko called and started running. Not away, but towards the shrieking. We followed him with our shields ready to be switched on. Within a few minutes, we were dodging every animal I had ever seen in the woods and more that were new to me. Maybe in the future, I would have a chance to get to know them.

A pack of wolves headed towards Cahir. They stopped for a brief moment and then continued on past us. I heard Cahir's thoughts. Hearing Cahir in my mind was another thing I hadn't told anyone yet. After I woke up from seeing the Oracle, I could feel Cahir in my mind, and with a bit of concentration, I could see through his eyes. Although I knew I would only be able to do that when he let me. He controlled the switch that showed me what he was seeing. It was like a camera in his head, or back in Earth like a Go Pro. He turned it on or off.

It was another example of how Erda and Earth were different. In Erda, they didn't need a piece of equipment to do things. They didn't need cars, computers, phones, or cameras. Somehow in Erda, they knew the source and tapped into it.

I was getting closer to feeling it in the same way. I only hoped it would be in time.

"There are only a few Shrieks up ahead. Cahir thinks that somehow they were separated from the pack, or perhaps they are scouts," I yelled to the group.

No one asked how I knew that. Everyone just accepted it. I realized that Princess Kara Beth must have always talked with wolves, or at least Cahir. That I remembered was probably wonderful news for them, but what was happening was more critical.

"It could also be a trap," Link said to all of us. "We haven't heard of individual Shrieks separating from the group before, so be careful."

We were already closer than anyone had been to a Shriek without being incapacitated. But we had to get close enough to see the Shrieks to blast their sound back to them.

Teddy and his friends had given us each one more thing before we beamed up: specially made noise-canceling headphones that they called ear muffs.

The ear muffs deadened the decibels of the shrieking, but we could still hear each other talking. However, once we got close enough to shoot, the shrieking would be almost intolerable.

But the ear muffs would deaden the sound enough to aim the shield and shoot. That was the plan anyway.

Forty-Two

"Something about this doesn't feel right to me," James said. For the past hour, James and his men from the village had been traveling through the woods on the outskirts of the core group.

But almost as soon as Niko told us to move forward after hearing the Shrieks in the distance, James had taken up a position on my left side with Zeid on my right. I was not going to protest their protection. Beru was directly in front of me, and Aki was behind me with John, Kit, Mark, and Thomas. Niko and Ruta were leading us.

I couldn't see Pita and his brothers, but I never could. All I knew is that they were there somewhere.

The Priscillas had flown off into the woods. I was terrified for them. They had no protection. But I couldn't call them back. They weren't listening to me. Why had they gone? Did I make them that mad? When they returned, I was going to have to apologize profusely to Pris. I held the word "when" to myself as tightly as I could. Not if. When.

"What do you mean?" I asked James.

We had slowed our running to a fast stealth walk, trying not to make any noise and alert the Shrieks. We didn't have any idea what they could hear. Maybe nothing. Maybe everything. We had so little knowledge about what the shrieks could do it was terrifying.

"Something. Can't put my finger on it," James replied.

I thought about what I could do if I could see more all the time and then asked a question that I had been pondering since the first time I pressed the star on my necklace.

"James," I asked, "you know what happens when I press your daughter's star, don't you?"

"She has told me."

"Can you see that way, too. Can everyone?"

"No, I can't. And no, not everyone can. It's a talent, a gift. Some people have that one, but not many. You are one. My daughter knew that you have it. She also knew that you didn't remember, so she gave you the necklace."

"Doesn't she need it anymore?"

"If she gave it to you, it's either because she can see without it, or because Liza wants you to be safe."

"She wants to make sure you are safe too, James."

"Agreed. And I still feel there is something wrong."

I jogged ahead a little and told Niko what James had said. Without a second thought, Niko raised his hand, and we all stopped. It felt as if everything paused, as if even the trees were holding their breaths.

We could hear the Shrieks in the distance. They were closer than before, but not yet loud enough to stun. We looked at each other, waiting.

Then nothing. The forest became silent as a tomb. Nothing moved. As we stood there, frozen, it felt as if we were the only ones left in the woods. All the animals, birds, and insects that could get away had gone behind us. They were counting on us to stop the noise.

But the noise had stopped without us doing anything. There

were no more shrieking sounds. Had the Shrieks turned away? Gone back? Why would they do that? Where had they gone?

Professor Link was quiet. There was nothing to do but wait.

Suzanne, as Lady, was flying high above us, staying away from the Shrieks that could bring her down in a second. Still, she could see what we couldn't see. Lady and her friends were our eyes in the air. She circled lower and lower, looking. On our common channel, Suzanne told us that she could see nothing other than the mass movement of forest life behind us. They were all waiting too. Probably wondering if they could return.

Suzanne said she could see the Riff in the distance, but no Shrieks. Not even the few we thought we had heard. Yes, she agreed, something was wrong. There were Shrieks, and now there weren't. What were we missing?

I switched my thought to Cahir, and he showed me what he saw. Trees and plants, but nothing that could move. He was circling us, widening the circle and he still saw nothing. I asked him to stop. Even though he was so quiet no one could hear him, I was worried. He might be moving into a trap. I tried not to think about the Priscillas.

There was no sound, only the rush of air in and out of our noses, although we did our best to muffle even that. Standing absolutely still was hard. My muscles started trembling, and I wondered how much longer I would be able not to move.

"Stay still," Link commanded.

And then we all heard it. Something so quiet an insect crawling on the ground would have been louder.

We moved in a circle, our backs to each other, looking for what was out there, and seeing nothing.

Niko motioned for us to make sure our ear muffs were on and raise our shields. I pressed the star on my neck and almost screamed at what I saw.

A split second later the forest exploded with sound, and shrieking green mouths surrounded us.

If I had ever been afraid before, it couldn't match what I felt in that moment. I held the match of anger to my terror, flipped the mirror switch, and fired.

Forty-Three

It got worse. The Shrieking. We reflected their shrieks back at them, and they screamed louder. I swear they grew bigger too. It became harder and harder to stay conscious. The noise was excruciating.

We were invisible behind our shields, but I had no idea how long the shields would hold up, or keep firing. This was different then our practicing underground. Besides, having the mirrors on this long was dangerous. What was Abbadon seeing?

The only positive effect that I could see from our effort was that the Shrieks were not advancing. Our tight circle held. Back to back, we shuffled sideways together. Each shuffle gave us a chance to re-trigger and fire at a new target. Plus moving helped us stay conscious. I could feel James' shoulder attached to me on the left, and Zeid's on the right. We held each other up. Feeling them there kept me firing, hoping that the next shot would stop the Shrieks.

Each step sideways revealed yet another huge open mouth to point our weapon at and fire into. I was grateful that there were no other creatures behind them that we could hurt in the process.

Then I noticed two things I almost wished I couldn't see.

Right before the Shrieks appeared, I had pushed the star. It seemed as if it was the best time possible to do such a thing. It was why Liza gave it to me, to keep us safe.

That shift in the way I could see around me showed me something terrible. With every shot we took the trees took the hit too. The sound was wounding the trees. Ferns that grew at their base had already withered. At that moment we were killing the innocent. I didn't know what to do but keep firing and praying when it was over we could heal them.

I pushed the sorrow away because what I could also see was another wave of Shrieks behind the first one. Their mouths open, they were shrieking too.

No wonder it was getting louder. There were more!

I sent the image of the outside circles of Shrieks to everyone. I kept the picture of the dying trees and plants to myself. For now. Because if we didn't stop these Shrieks here, Shatterskin would be right behind and destroy everything anyway. Forever. Then there would be nothing to heal. It would be gone.

Teddy had shown us how we could widen our firing beam if we needed to. It was a dangerous move because there was even more of a possibility that people or other creatures would be killed if we missed.

But in this case, the Shrieks had done us a favor by circling us, obviously not caring anymore if they killed each other, and we had applied one of Niko's lessons of standing together as one. There was no chance of us hitting each other while we were in a circle together. It gave us a huge advantage.

We widened our shooting beams, and that made a difference. The lessening of the shrieking told us that it was working. Although still standing, if being a green blob can qualify as standing, what was coming out of their mouths was at an increasingly lower decibel.

Finally, there was silence. We had stunned the Shrieks with their own sounds. I sent a huge thank you to Teddy and his crew out into the universe. That part had worked. But now what? How long would they stay stunned?

Then there was the next phase. Would it work? We knew even less about the effect of what we were going to do next because there had been no way to test it. Teddy and his crew had to guess what made up the Shrieks.

They had taken the little information that they had about how the Shrieks moved through the country and made a few educated guesses. We were ready to try out a few of them. Hopefully, at least one would work before they recovered.

We left the ear muffs on, just in case. Shields were turned off and slung over our backs. We didn't need them for the next stage, but no one wanted to be without them.

Each of us was wearing a backpack, but instead of clothes inside of them, we had bags of salt. Big bags. And containers of water. Since the Shrieks appeared to bypass areas of increased salt, like around what in Earth is known as Salt Lake City, we were hoping they did that because salt was not good for them.

They also stayed away from bodies of water. Could it be like the Wicked Witch of the West and they could also be dissolved by water? That seemed too simplistic, but we were all ready to try anything.

We stayed in our circle, backs to each other in case we needed to fire again. But we expanded our circle until each of us was standing directly in front of a green blob.

Close up that blob was even scarier. I thought that all its sounds came from the large open hole that we called a mouth. It wasn't really a mouth. These blobs didn't eat. They only shrieked.

However, what we found as we looked at them up close was

that their entire body was covered with little openings. Their whole being was made to project sound.

Niko was staring closely at his Shriek. So close it was terrifying. If it started shrieking, Niko was probably dead.

"Okay. Salt first. Then add the water if nothing happens," Niko said. "I don't need to tell you that we don't have that much with us, so don't run out. There are more Shrieks here than we thought there would be."

My expanded vision had faded. The star seemed only to be able to hold me there for short periods of time. But I didn't need it to see the Shrieks. Perhaps because they were stunned, they were all visible now. To everyone. At least a hundred Shrieks surrounded us. Not just the few that we thought we were chasing. How they managed to fool us was a question we would have to face, but this was not the time.

It was the time to get rid of them. I took a deep breath, praying we were getting ready to kill the Shrieks and not wake them up.

In one hand we each held a container of salt, and in the other, a bottle of water. I looked at Zeid. His azure eyes flared, and we turned together and poured.

Forty-Four

The Shrieks started moving. We kept pouring, working only with the inner circle. The outer ring of Shrieks remained frozen.

"Don't stop," Professor Link commanded. "If they are not making a sound, it might be working."

I wanted to be a smart ass and say, "You aren't here. You don't see these things moving around."

It finally dawned on me that they were swelling, not moving. The Shrieks were getting bigger and bigger. What if it opened its mouth? Could we survive it?

And then one of the Shrieks burst. Totally, totally gross. Green stuff everywhere. After the first Shriek burst, we stepped away and let the rest of the first ring of Shrieks burst without green goo hitting anyone.

Now that we knew it worked, we moved to the second ring and started pouring. Pour. Swell. Step away. Burst.

What seemed like hours later, but must have been only a few minutes, we were out of salt. But there were still five Shrieks left.

"Try the water," Link said.

Aki poured the last bit of water on them while the rest of us prepared for explosions of green blobs. Nothing happened. Well, something happened. The Shrieks started moving again. Not swelling this time. Instead, their mouths began opening. Most of us had taken our ear muffs off, and they were hanging around our necks. We slapped them back on, and Aki fired her shield at all of five of the Shrieks as fast as she could.

After what seemed an eternity they were frozen once more. Mouths open. Ready to scream.

"Now what? We are out of salt and water. Plus green blobs are lying all over the ground. What's to say that they won't rise again? We need to get rid of it all," I said.

"Time to try the other thing we talked about," I heard Link say.

"What other thing?" Zeid asked. Well everyone asked as they turned to me expecting me to do something. Zeid was just the one who said it out loud.

They thought it was me who knew? It wasn't. I had no idea what Link was talking about.

I had no other thing to do. Whatever magic I had was still hidden from me. Other than the time I fired lightning bolts from my hands, and I didn't have the foggiest idea of how I did that.

Besides, like everyone else I was exhausted. Even if I knew where my magic was keeping itself, I didn't know how I would dredge up enough energy to carry it out.

"Spit on them?" I asked.

When everyone looked at me blankly, I said, "Spit is water and some salt right? It's stupid but worth a try."

Shrugging, Zeid stepped forward and spat on the nearest Shriek. Everyone laughed. It was totally stupid.

"Okay, it's stupid, but it feels great. Give it a try."

We spread out and started spitting on the still standing Shrieks. Zeid was right. It felt awesome, but nothing happened. Probably not enough salt.

Good thing it was only us watching what we were doing.

"Listen," James said. Once again we paused and listened. Rustling. And laughing. Priscillas!

Flying straight for me were Pris, Cil, and La, laughing so hard they were wavering as they flew.

"Oh ziffer and zut!" Pris said. "That's the silliest thing I ever saw. Spitting on green blobs. Had to be your idea, Hannah."

As happy as I was to see Pris, I wanted to tug her pigtails extra hard. Instead, I said, "Try it, you'll like it."

The three fairies hovered over one Shriek and spat. Well, if a tiny drop of water could be called spitting.

"You're right, Kara," La said. "That feels great, but we have something we think you will like better."

The rustling noise increased, and the Priscilla's gestured to what looked like a moving mass of earth.

"What the ziffer is that?" John yelled.

"The next thing to try," Cil said. "But, you might want to get off the ground. They might not know the difference between your feet and a green blob."

Everyone took a look at the brown mass moving towards them and started running to the nearest tree. I swear the branches had lowered themselves, so we all were able to grab a limb and swing up off the ground. Except for Aki who simply levitated herself up into the tree. *I am going to have to get her to teach me how to do that,* I thought.

We watched from the safety of the trees as the mass came closer. Now we could see it was thousands and thousands of insects—not any I had seen before though.

"What are those?" I asked alternately horrified and thrilled as they swarmed over every green blog and started eating it. A large group split off and took the remaining five blobs, swarming over them until we couldn't see them anymore.

Within minutes the blobs were gone, and the ground was cleaned of every bit of green. However, the insects appeared to be thoroughly searching for every molecule that was left, so we all stayed in the trees.

Lady had flown down and watched the insects and was perched in a tree with us. I thought she was looking a little hungry. Insects, yum, good. The Priscillas were swinging off a twig looking as casual as if it was merely another beautiful fall day.

"These are our friends," La said.

"Your friends?"

"Yes. Excellent friends!"

"Where did they come from?" I asked.

The Priscillas didn't answer. It was Link who filled us in as we sat on tree branches watching our new brown insect friends make sure there was nothing left of the Shrieks.

"This is where the Priscillas have been going at night," Link said. "These insect friends don't live in this region. They had to be convinced to be brought here to fight the Shrieks. It was the Priscillas who did all the work.

"We knew we couldn't bring them in until the Shrieks were stopped, and we still weren't sure it would work. But Pris had heard of these little buggers, excuse the pun, who could eat anything, digest it, and not get sick. It was worth a try, and it seems to have been very effective."

We all looked at the newly cleaned forest floor and agreed that it was a brilliant idea. I had a lot of apologizing to do.

"How did you get them here," Aki asked, always the practical one.

"In Sound Bubbles," Link answered.

Complete silence reigned as we all contemplated what bubbles filled with crawling brown insects must have looked like flying over Erda.

Once again, Aki asked the practical question.

"Where will they be living?"

Link's laughter was not all that reassuring.

Forty-Five

Just as I thought, the Whistle Pigs and Ginete had been there all along. Teddy and Pita popped up again out of nowhere, strolling through the woods as if they didn't have a care in the world. They took in the picture of all of us sitting in trees, and a mat of brown insects on the ground as if it was a regular, everyday occurrence.

At Teddy and Pita's arrival, the insects all moved over to another part of the forest and stayed there. Seeing that it was safe, we came down out of the trees to meet them. It was only then that I realized that I had not seen Ruta hop into a tree. I spun around looking for him.

"Looking for Ruta?" Niko asked me. Niko looked as if nothing had happened in the last few hours. He was alert and unrumpled.

Unlike me. I hoped that I didn't look as bad as I felt, but at the narrowing of Niko's eyes, I had a feeling that I looked, and smelled, fairly bad.

Niko flicked his gaze over to one of the bigger trees outside the clearing where we had fought the Shrieks and said, "He probably went that way."

I had no idea what Niko was talking about. "What way? Is

he still walking?"

"No, he left by tree," Niko said.

"Are we doing that kind of riddle, like 'who's on first?'" I asked. "He left by tree? And while we are talking about where and how people come and go, where did the two of you come from, Teddy and Pita?"

Teddy grinned, probably thinking it was friendly, but his grins were always slightly terrifying with those two big teeth in the front meeting the equally large teeth from the bottom. I tried not to think about what would happen if he decided to nibble my hand.

"Well, if we're saying it Niko's way, we came by ground," Teddy said pointing into the woods where I saw more Whistle Pigs arriving carrying something that reminded me of a pet carrier, but much bigger.

"So if you arrived by ground and Ruta left by tree, where is he now?"

"Probably already at the meeting room we have prepared for you. We brought water for bathing too." Teddy said, not so subtly.

"And food?" I asked.

When Teddy nodded yes I didn't waste any time getting to the area where the circles appeared to be, but once I got there, I had no idea how to make it work. Everyone else seemed to know how. They stepped on one, and swoosh they were gone.

I caught Pita and Teddy laughing. Standing on the circle, hands on my hips trying to look commanding, I said, "Are you messing with me?"

Before I could get the words me out of my mouth, I was already underground, and Pita and Teddy were still laughing at me. But now we were all standing in another vast room that seemed to be just like the one we had left. I wondered if it was the same one, and this was all an illusion.

"Well," Pris said, "Yes, in many ways all of this that we are experiencing is an illusion, but not the kind you mean. So no, this is not the same room. And no, you can't apologize right now. We have to go make sure our insect friends are being taken care of."

With a haughty flick of her head, Pris flew off. Cil and La looked as if they would have liked to stay, but Pris gave them one of her famous "get over here before I tear your head off" looks and with an apologetic glance at me, followed their big sister.

"Go get cleaned up everyone," Niko said. "We'll meet in the food hall in an hour."

Niko didn't have to add that we had a problem, or two, or three. But at that moment we were safe, and dirty, tired, and hungry.

Once the Ginete explained to us that the tunnels and rooms where we were now were patterned exactly like the ones we left, none of us had trouble figuring out which way to go to get to our rooms.

Pita walked with me to my room and waited for me to say what was on my mind before opening the door for me.

"Where were you?" I asked Pita.

"We traveled beneath you. We are not fighters in the same way that you are. We provide what you need. Partnering with our cousins, the Whistle Pigs, we can do things we could never do on our own, and of course, a little magic never hurts. Think of us as the Red Cross in Erda. Well, not exactly, but close. Maybe a cross between them and your ministers. No, not that …"

Pita stopped as I laid my hand on his arm. "Thank you. That's not what I meant, Pita. My words don't come out right some of the time. No, most of the time. Your being here is the best thing I could think of. What would we do if you didn't have this space for us? I was just worried for you and Teddy, and all of your families."

Pita's golden eyes sparkled with tears as he opened the door for me. I didn't want to embarrass him, so I pretended not to notice.

As I walked in the door, I thought of something else. "If the Ginete and the Whistle Pigs are sorta like the Red Cross and Faith ministers, does that mean you have healers too."

This time Pita laughed. At least I think it was a laugh.

"Of course we do. What do you think happened in that ceremony we did for you back at the Castle?"

"A healing?"

"A healing of sorts and it's still in process. But to answer the rest of your question, yes, there are healers that work on physical injuries, if they are not too serious. Sometimes, no one can help."

Pita took another look at me and said, "Oh. You're asking about the trees and plants that were injured today, aren't you?

"That is something that will be on the agenda at the meeting. Go ahead, get cleaned up, I'll wait here for you."

After Pita closed the door on me, I looked at the closed door for a long time. I thought about how Beru would shut the door at the Castle, lock it, and then stand guard. Here, Pita did the same.

What was there to guard against? What were they protecting me from here in this safe space? Or, since I heard the door lock, perhaps they were protecting themselves from me?

I shook my head. That was ridiculous. I was not dangerous at all, except for the way I looked and smelled. But that was easy to take care of. I decided to worry about the rest later.

Forty-Six

"We have a problem," Niko said.

"Not like we don't know it," John huffed. Behind him, the other men from the village agreed with him with grunts and agreements of "Yea, we do!"

I felt terrible for them. These men had left their families to come help us. Now it looked as if our solution for killing the Shrieks might not work, and what we did might have made everything worse because Abbadon now knew what we intended to do.

"Sure, we managed to stun them and then dissolve most of them, but at what cost?" Kit added.

It was the first time I had heard Kit speak up in a meeting. Up until now, he'd gone along with whatever Niko said, but something had triggered his fear to the point he had gotten over his shyness.

I knew what it was, but I waited until someone else said it.

Niko continued after acknowledging John and Kit, but not answering them directly. "Before we go down the rabbit hole of what didn't work, let's acknowledge what did," Niko said.

"We worked!" Pris sang as she fluttered down on to the center of the table and did a little pirouette.

Her performance prompted a round of clapping, which I was sure was exactly what she was aiming for. But she was right. Their insect brigade did work. I clapped as hard as I could to let her know how proud I was of her. Pris was still peeved at me, and I missed her. I hoped she would get over it soon.

We were all seated around another large table just like the one we left behind. I thought about how much the Ginete and the Whistle Pigs had to do to be ready for us this way. There had to be some serious magic going on that enabled the cousins to not only dig the tunnels but furnish them for us too in such a short time.

Cil whispered in my ear, "These tunnels and rooms have been here forever, Hannah. They are not building them as you move.

"What they do is add the portals that will bring you down here. Once you move on, they'll remove the portals, so the wrong people, or things, don't trigger them. Like the Shrieks."

Cil shivered when she said that, and so did I. The idea that the Shrieks might be able to come into this safe place scared me too.

"Thank you, Cil," I whispered. "You saved me from making an even bigger fool of myself."

I wondered how long Pita and Teddy would have let me continue to believe that they were that fast. Fooling the new girl. I caught Pita's eyes, and he winked a big golden eye at me! The nerve.

"Some people say it's better to believe anything is possible than to have a closed mind, Hannah," Niko said. "Don't be too hard on yourself. It's better that you have an open mind than one that can't accept a new idea."

Speaking to the entire group, Niko added. "And that is what we are all going to need—a belief in possibilities. I'm serious about looking at what worked. Until a few weeks ago, we didn't have a single weapon against the Shrieks. Now we do."

"Sure. But how is that going to work in a bigger picture? How are we going to be able to carry enough salt and water to dissolve the Shrieks?" John asked.

"That's not all. How are you planning to transport insects everywhere? That's not counting the fact that the trees and plants took a huge hit from both the sound that was blasted towards them and the salt that was dumped on the ground."

When Niko started to answer, John held up his hand.

"Let me finish. There are not enough of us to stun and then dissolve the hundreds and hundreds of Shrieks that will be attacking us next time.

"And even if you solve these problems, we have huge ones that I don't see any solution for. How did the Shrieks know we were coming? How did they hide from us? And finally, the biggest problem of all, to do what we did, the mirrors were left on for a long time.

"The possibility that Abbadon knows what we did is huge. And he probably saw what worked and what didn't work and he will use all that against us."

"And," Kit added. "He knows where we are right now!"

Niko paused. "Does anyone else have any concerns that they want to voice?"

When no one else said anything, Niko said. "Thank you, John and Kit for bringing up all the problems that we need to address. But we will solve them."

"Because we have to," James added. "If we don't, we don't have a chance. I know that we all miss our families, and want to go home, but if we don't figure this out, there won't be a home to go back to. If we want our wives and children to be safe, we can't give up."

John looked at his brother and nodded. He didn't look happy, but what James said was true. There really was no choice. We had to solve the problems and do it fast because John was also correct. If Abbadon knew where we were right now, wouldn't he target us first?

"Okay," Niko said. "One problem at a time. Which one first?"

"We have a solution for one of them," Teddy spoke up. "We were already working on the issue of salt and water. We just needed to see if it worked at all. Now that we know it does, we only had to solve getting more water and salt faster. That turned out to be easier than we thought."

"But won't a huge amount of salt destroy the plant life?" John asked.

"Yes, it could," Teddy said. "However, we have addressed this issue in two ways. More plain water after it's over to flush the salt down into the ground as far as we can get it. And the trees had been working with us to develop a counter to the salt once it gets deep enough for their roots to deal with it."

"You've been working with the trees?" I asked.

"And what delivery system could possibly be big enough?" John demanded.

A huge blast of air blew through the open door, and Earl walked into the room accompanied by Ruta.

Niko turned to the two of them and said, "Great timing. It's your turn now."

Forty-Seven

Earl was imposing as ever, and Ruta, who always reminded me of a tree stump with arms and legs, walked into the room together. They were an interesting pair.

Earl didn't give us any time to wonder what they were doing there; he strode to the head of the table and stared at us. His hair streamed down his back flowing like a gray river. Earl had a face that looked as if it had remained that way for thousands of years, unchanging. Now that I knew more about Erda, it was possible that was true.

Earl looked at me and smiled. "I see you have learned a little bit, Hannah. You know your name now, and you're beginning to grow into it. Still trying to remember your magic though. Although that little display of lightning bolts from your hands was a nice prelude. Do you know how you did it yet?"

I shook my head no and then asked, "Am I the only one who doesn't know your true name, Earl?"

Earl looked around the room taking in our team. We were all so different. His gaze rested on Suzanne, and she smiled back at him.

"Well, they've heard of me, as have you, Kara Beth. But not everyone knows me as Coro, the commander of storms."

I could tell who hadn't known who he was, because most of the table, like me, gasped. The Priscillas, on the other hand, were now adorning his coat. No fear there.

Earl smiled down at them, and they all looked up at him adoringly. "Yes, some of us have been friends a long time," Earl said, and then his massive hands carefully patted each fairy on her head. If I had done that they might have chewed off my fingers. When Earl did it, I think they actually purred.

Suzanne spoke. "Earl, as Coro, is our delivery system. My father will sweep up waters from the oceans. He'll carry the salt water to where you are fighting the Shrieks. My mother will assist him in directing the water to only the Shrieks and not dumping it on you, at least as much as possible."

"Your mother? Who is your mother? Where is your mother?" I asked, totally confused.

"My mother is Ariel. She is the leader of the winds. I fly with her every day. She prefers to be the wind over being locked into a physical body, but I am sure she will be present as herself for you one day, Kara Beth."

I had to force myself to listen to what Suzanne said after that. Was I going to return to my family? Did she mean Hannah's family or Kara Beth's family? I suspected it was my Erda family that she was referring to, and at that moment I realized I still didn't remember them.

"Let it go, Kara Beth," Suzanne said. "It will happen soon enough, but only after we have completed this part of our mission."

When I still looked puzzled, she added, "Get a grip, Hannah. We are here to deal with the Shrieks and Shatterskin."

"You said 'this part of our mission.' What other parts are there?"

For a moment Suzanne's face softened. Perhaps she hadn't

meant to tell me that. "This is enough to think about for now."

John, who seemed to have taken over being the spokesman for the men from the village said, "Okay. Earl here brings the salt water, and his wife dumps it on the Shrieks. Let's say that works. What happens to the salt?"

Ruta stepped to the head of the table. Aki took one look at him and somehow levitated him up high enough so all of us could see him. He gave her a grateful look before speaking. "After the Shrieks have been killed and devoured by the Priscillas' insect friends, the trees will take care of the rest. They have developed a supplemental root system that will pull the salt out of the soil, and then release minerals from the salt that are beneficial back into the ground.

"After the roots have absorbed all the excess salt, the trees will release the supplemental roots that are storing the salt water. Those roots will drop down into the underground streams and eventually the streams will carry those roots to the ocean. Over time, the roots will dissolve and return the salt to where it came from."

"Seriously?" I said. "This is all going to happen this way? Are you kidding? How do the trees know how to do that?"

"You mean you have a harder time believing that the trees have intelligence and understanding than you do that Earl is the commander of the storms and his wife of the wind? Aren't you saying then that people are smarter than nature? Especially trees?" Ruta demanded.

"Well, if you put it that way," I began, but Ruta wasn't done. I swear I thought I saw smoke come out of his head.

"Look around you, smart girl. What's holding these rooms together? Yes, tree roots. What are you breathing? Air. Who put it there and took out what you can't breathe? Trees. You live because trees have made this world habitable for you and every other form of life. Where does all this magic come from? You can't even remember. But guess. It's not hard. Trees, Hannah. Trees."

Everybody had been staring at Ruta. When he was done, all heads swiveled to me. I stood there rooted in my seat not knowing what to say. I was furious. I let the anger build. I allowed myself to feel what it felt like to be powerless, to be called a little girl, to know that I was failing my friends. I heard Link say, "That's it, Hannah. Control it. Now surrender."

I did what he said. I surrendered to everything that Ruta had said. I surrendered to my helplessness. I surrendered to who I could be. As I did, the anger turned to something else, and within me rose a massive surge of power as the door to my memory opened and the past rushed out.

Forty-Eight

The table and everyone around it faded into the background. I was alone and yet not alone. Shadows and images of the past surrounded me. I let the memories of the past seep into me. From the ground beneath me, I felt the heartbeat of the earth.

Around me, I could feel the pulsing from the tree roots that made up the walls, floors, and ceiling of the room. The trees heard everything. They knew everything. They stored all our memories within their bodies. Even in what appeared as death, they remained in different forms. Their fire warmed us. The smoke eventually returned to earth and fed the next generation of trees. Trees that fell in the forest provided homes and food for thousands of beings that lived in harmony with them.

Trees breathed in and out. They transformed every form of energy into something that was useful. They were the breath and life of the world.

The past sat on the edge of my vision waiting for me to acknowledge it. I let it in.

In my mind's eye, I saw the stretch of a long meadow that ended at the base of a tall hill. Beru and I were playing together.

The Priscillas were dancing on the top of flowers singing and laughing over the antics of their insect friends. Ruta stood at the edge of the meadow, just at the tree line. Watching. Protecting. It was glorious. We were all happy without a care in the world.

Suddenly a wind rose from the west, and five runners burst out of the woods and into the meadow. Long legs were heading towards our home in the village. They were messengers from the Castle. I recognized Niko leading the way. Lady swooped out of the trees and headed the same way as the runners. We knew something terrible was happening. Beru, Ruta, and I ran as fast as we could to follow them, the Priscillas flying ahead of us.

We arrived out of breath and just in time to hear the name of Abbadon for the first time. Abbadon the destroyer was on the move. The King's brother had decided that what he had was not enough. Abbadon wanted more. He wanted it all. Niko described the Shrieks. My mother screamed. My father reached over and held her hand as Niko continued to tell of the destruction. First the shrieking, then the shattering of every living thing. Every village in the Shrieks' path had been destroyed. Most of the West Coast was brown and dead.

My vision cleared and I was back in our meeting room—everyone silent, waiting for me. I felt like throwing up. I wanted to run and scream from the room.

But the time of running was over. I knew everyone had seen the memories played out before me, and were waiting for me to ask the next question. I could feel a surge of support from Aki. She had done it before for me in our practice sessions, when I wanted to give up.

Those practice sessions back in the Castle seemed as if they had been a lifetime ago, not just a few weeks. So much had changed. I had remembered.

I asked, "How long ago was that, Niko?"

"In Erda time, just two years. A few lifetimes in Earth time. As soon as your parents, the King and Queen, heard about what we had seen, they didn't hesitate. They were afraid to lose you, so they sent you through the portal to the Earth Realm. You know that Suzanne was given charge over you, so we had reports about your life almost on a daily basis.

"We loved hearing about how happy you were, and we were all willing for you to stay. But then Abbadon got better at what he was doing, and Suzanne thought you might be able to turn the tide in our favor. By then, your parents didn't have a say in the matter.

"We needed you. We didn't know you would have forgotten everything. We thought you would be ready as soon as you returned. At first, we were devastated, thinking that perhaps we should have left you in Earth. But now that you were here, we had to give it a chance."

I know if I had a mirror to look at my face I would have seen that it had turned white, drained of blood. What could I do, now?

"Two years and all this destruction? Just two years of your time?"

The awareness of what Abbadon was doing overflowed into my veins, bringing the blood rushing back. I opened myself and reached out trying to feel the connection to the magic that I knew I had. It was time to remember. It was time for me to stop fighting my destiny.

I stood up. I felt my connection to the trees. The trees that had been trying to tell me something ever since I had arrived. It was their power that flowed in my veins. I rooted myself in their embrace, an embrace that reached into every surface of the earth.

I lifted my internal sight to the ground above us, where parts of the trees that grew in air stood, patiently providing. I saw Cahir guarding the circles that would bring us up to the forest floor. His gold eyes flashed as I entered his mind, with his permission.

He showed me that the trees were drooping, bark peeling away, limbs barely attached. I remembered that I could help. I could heal the trees. I sent out a pulse of energy through the ground, through the roots into the trees above. I directed it into every tree affected by what we had done.

Through Cahir's eyes, I watched the return of the trees' lifeblood flowing through every branch. Repairing breaks and healing scars.

No more little girl trying to remember her magic. I remembered. I knew that I was still weak from lack of practice, but I knew who I was, Princess Kara Beth.

I returned my vision to the room and to the people who had been watching around the table who had waited for me to return to Erda and then to myself.

"Thank you, Ruta, for always watching over me." Taking each person in, I looked into each face treasuring what I saw there.

"I remember all of you now. I also remember this."

On my open palm, a ball of light danced. My magic. A gift from the trees. The Priscillas shrieked with joy and flew up into my hair. Even Pris kissed me on the cheek. Ruta smiled proudly. The five men from the village hugged each other.

Earl clapped, breaking the celebration. "Congratulations, Kara Beth. But don't get too cocky. You haven't remembered everything. But now, with what you do remember we can fight and win. Abbadon has sent a wall of Shrieks to our location. They will be here soon.

"Even with all our magic, we may not succeed. Abbadon has learned some tricks with his Shrieks. And after watching the last battle, he will have more ways to deceive us."

Looking around the room, Earl asked, "Are you ready?"

"Ready!" we all shouted.

In my head, I heard the nursery rhyme I had played in Earth. "Ready or not, here we come."

I hoped it was the Shrieks and Shatterskin who were not ready. We'd find out soon enough.

Forty-Nine

"Except me," Zeid said after everyone else had left the room. We had both stayed behind because he knew my secret. When I had looked around the room, I saw Zeid sitting beside Suzanne and Beru. I looked straight at him, pretended that I knew him, and moved on.

But it had been a lie. I didn't remember Zeid, and he knew it too. I could see the pain in his eyes. I wanted to remember. I just couldn't.

There was nothing to say. I wasn't doing it on purpose. But that didn't make it hurt any less for Zeid. I could at least feel that. There was something between us, something important, but the memory of it was hidden from me.

"Is it because of this?" Zeid said lifting my left arm and revealing my friendship bracelet from Johnny. I remembered Johnny. But my life that included Johnny felt like a dream from another lifetime.

A lifetime when I had been just a young girl and Johnny had been a young man who had only begun to suspect how I felt about him. Johnny lived in a world without Shrieks. Without a monster called Abbadon who intended to destroy every living thing.

When I lived in the Earth Realm, I knew of evil people. Johnny and I had escaped more than once from men that had wanted to harm us. But it was nothing like what was happening in Erda.

The crush I had on Johnny felt just like that now. A schoolgirl crush. But maybe the memory of that crush, kept me wearing the bracelet, and made me feel guilty when I looked at Zeid. Perhaps I had closed the door on who Zeid was to me, because of Johnny.

Zeid dropped my arm but continued to hold my hand. We stood face to face only a few inches apart. Even though I didn't remember Zeid from before, he pulled at me. I wanted to stand there looking into his eyes that reminded me of the ocean until all of the nightmares of Abbadon faded away.

It was Zeid who broke our eye contact. "Stay safe, Kara Beth. It doesn't matter that you don't remember, because I do."

Zeid dropped my hand and left the room without looking back. My heart sank. I should have told him to stay safe too—so many things I should have done and didn't.

I didn't have long to wallow in regret because Pris flew in the door and pulled my hair. "Stop it!" she said. "Bring your ziffering magic and let's go. You don't have time to be mooning around after Zeid or anyone else for that matter."

After pulling my hair, Pris switched to my earlobe and dragged me towards the door. For a tiny thing, Pris had a lot of strength and determination. I followed. She was right. I had no time to be trying to figure out who Zeid was to me. Besides, there was no way I was going to get Pris mad at me again.

Niko had assigned everyone with something specific to do. He had given us an hour to get it done. Even though no one wore watches, everyone always appeared on time or finished in time.

Once I was late to a meeting, and Aki had spent our next two sessions teaching me how to access time internally which is where she said it resided anyway.

There were only forty-five minutes left before we were heading to the surface. But Niko's assignment to me was different. I was to go into the meditation room and be quiet. Listen. "Get back to listening, Hannah," he had said.

Calling me Hannah was probably a signal to me. As Hannah, I had been good at listening to my internal guide. The disorientation I faced when I returned to Erda had thrown me off, and listening had not been high on my priority list. Now it had to be. Niko had said so, and I could see Aki nodding in assent.

I almost rolled my eyes at him, and then stopped halfway through the roll. We both pretended that it hadn't happened. Even with the eye rolling, I knew he was right.

"Okay, okay," I yelled at Pris who wouldn't let go. "I'm going right now."

"Better. I have to go feed our insect friends."

"Where are they?"

"In a big room. You don't want to go in there though. They're everywhere. We'll have them right behind you to clean up after you all dissolve the Shrieks."

Pris flew off down the hall. Her wings sparkled in the light of the tunnel. Now I knew that it was the trees that were providing the light source. They used a portion of their energy to glow where a light was needed. When light wasn't, they automatically turned themselves off.

As I walked the hall to the room, I asked the trees to dim their light, and I slowed both my walking and my breath. I didn't need to wait to get to the room to listen. I could listen while I walked.

With each step, I opened myself to hear what to do. The Oracle had taught me how to reach her, and I opened myself to her. The return of my memory was due in large part to what had happened in that room.

Now I asked what I needed to know and to give me the wisdom to do the right thing.

I was running even before I felt the first boom. In the transport room, Beru tossed me my shield, headset, and backpack. We were still taking our own supply of salt and water. No one wanted to be trapped with a Shriek while Coro was busy with another.

Within a split second of stepping onto our circles, we were on the surface. With our earmuffs set on high and shields in front, we advanced toward the sound. Not just shrieking. Shattering. The Riff had come to us.

Fifty

The surface was total chaos. Every living thing was trying to flee from the ear-splitting sounds that the Shrieks were making. But this time they had nowhere to go. They were trapped in an ever-narrowing box surrounded by Shrieks advancing on them.

Abbadon must have learned a new strategy to use with the Shrieks. Probably from watching the last battle through our mirror shields and how we had won it. His new plan appeared to be frighteningly effective. Hundreds of Shrieks were arriving from all four directions. All of them moving towards a center where they had trapped their prey.

They had abandoned the line moving through the forest, and instead, each massive column headed towards the center. Once they reached the center, everything would be dead, and maybe then they would advance again in a line, killing as they moved through the land.

Yes, that meant they were stunning themselves for a time when they shrieked at each other, but then the next line moved forward and took over. And there were lines upon lines of Shrieks ready to step in and take over.

The sound they fired at each other wasn't enough to stun them for long, and after a few minutes, they were moving again.

Relentlessly forward towards the center.

And that was the Shrieks that we could see. Now that we learned from the last battle that they had learned to be invisible to us, there was no telling how many Shrieks there were actually present.

At the last minute, Teddy and Pita had rerouted where we came to the surface, so instead of emerging in the middle of the converging Shrieks, we were on the outskirts of the line advancing from the east.

Even with our ear muffs turned on high the sound was almost paralyzing. My body wanted to shut down and stop moving, but I pushed forward, although I wasn't sure how long my strength would last.

At first, we ran in a line, spread out behind the East column until we got close enough for our next plan. I could feel everyone's distress. What was saving us was that the Shrieks' attention was towards the center, and so were their sound blasts.

We were receiving the residual sound which was bad enough. However, if the line we were chasing turned and fired at us, we knew we might not survive. The only chance we had was to keep blasting them before they knew we were there and turned around.

It was hard to watch what was happening with the trees. They were absorbing massive amounts of sound, attempting to soften the effects of it on the animals by taking the hit themselves. Now that I was aware of the trees as the breath and source of life on the planet, I knew that the trees taking such massive hits would have huge ramifications. We had to stop the shrieking as fast as possible to minimize the damage.

Teddy had altered the shields we were using while we were below and increased the magnification to one-thousand times. All of us thought that it was possible Abbadon might have modified the Shrieks to withstand the magnified sounds we had blasted at them, and we must have been right.

Even with the increased capacity of our shields, it took a concentrated time for each blast to stun the Shrieks in front of us, and at the same time, we were hurting the trees too.

I had to shut down a part of my feelings to keep going, and I knew everyone else was doing the same thing. Still, in spite of it all, I could feel the overarching support and love of the trees in spite of what we were doing to them. I knew they understood. It didn't make it any easier.

The Shrieks' increased capacity to withstand their own shrieking must have been how Abbadon could change the Shrieks battle plan. Besides, it was unlikely he cared whether they lived or died. They were only a tool, not living beings.

Even if they were, Abbadon wouldn't have cared. Killing everything was his goal in the end anyway. What were a few hundred dead Shrieks to him? He had already destroyed villages, people, and forests and everything that lived in them for thousands of miles.

We knew that there was no way for our small team to stop all the Shrieks Abbadon had created for this attack. It was as if he knew this was his last stand with the Shrieks.

What we had planned would work, I told myself. If we stopped the Shrieks here, we had a chance.

So even though it looked hopeless, we worked hard not to let that thought enter our minds. Instead, we focused on our strengths and what we could do in each moment. Professor Link was continually alerting us to what was happening. He was in contact with Lady and her dragon friends who were flying high above the battlefield. They had to stay out of range of the sound that the Shrieks would periodically blast at the sky.

We could see birds by the hundreds falling to the ground

every time the Shrieks swept their sound upward, and I prayed that Lady and her fellow dragons would be safe. But in order to see more, I knew that sometimes the dragons had to swoop down within range, putting them in danger.

Cahir and his friends were behind us, trying to find the end of the Shrieks' line, and providing a border that no animal crossed by mistake. Through his eyes, I could see how thick the range of Shrieks was, and it was only the continual encouragement of the rest of the team that kept me from feeling despair. That, and the awareness that there was no option for failure.

The Priscillas were still underground with the Ginete and Whistle Pigs, waiting with the Shriek-eating insects. They were all safe for now, but if Shatterskin got this far, they would be destroyed too. We could hear his booming in the distance and knew that we had a limited amount of time in which to work.

There were so many ways we could fail. Either the Shrieks would turn on us, our earmuffs or shields would stop working, or more Shrieks would arrive or were already present that we couldn't see. Then there was the chance that Coro and the storm would not get through or that one by one we would get picked off by a well-planned Shriek attack. These were the things that we knew could happen. What about the ones we didn't know about?

Because we knew we couldn't fight all those Shrieks, our focus was to create an escape path for the animals trapped in the center, and do it before we became incapacitated. Once that path was created, Coro would arrive with his drenching salt rain. We were praying that the Shrieks didn't need to be stunned to dissolve them.

I could hear James directing his men as Niko led the team through the opening in the line. Then Ruta and Aki followed, with Zeid, Beru and me behind them.

We were increasing the width of the path as we went. James and his team were keeping the path from closing behind us.

If we could keep our wits about us in the face of mounting pressure and impossible odds we had a chance. I had the star that Liza gave me that I could press if I needed to, but I was afraid if I saw what else was present I would succumb to fear. If all else failed, I would use it, but until then there was enough to deal with.

We were almost to the front of the line when I heard Link call out, "Behind you."

I turned to see that the men from the village were no longer there and the path that we had made was closing. We were trapped.

Fifty-One

I hesitated. If I fired, and James and his men were behind the line of Shrieks that I could see, I might kill the men.

"Help!" I said to Link. "I can't see James' men, and I'm afraid to fire."

This time I had a direct response from Lady. I had heard Suzanne in my head before, but never when she was a dragon, so it took me a second to recognize her voice.

I looked up as she swooped over our heads and the line of Shrieks, and then rose swiftly in the sky, just as the Shrieks turned to fire at her. I watched as she wobbled and then recovered.

"They are far behind the line with Cahir. They needed to move back because James was stunned. It's safe to fire on the Shrieks behind you, Kara."

All this took a matter of seconds, but it was enough time for a Shriek to be almost on top of me, his slimy hole filled green body practically touching mine as he opened his mouth. I screamed as I fired, again and again until the way behind us was clear again, and we were surrounded only by Shrieks that stood stunned or fallen.

The three of us looked at each other, and Zeid gave Beru

and me a thumbs up sign. Beru looked almost as green as the Shrieks. I knew she hated battle and would do almost anything not to be there. But Beru was courageous, and the one thing she would never do is not protect her friends if she could.

The ground began to shake, and I panicked thinking that Shatterskin had arrived, but instead it was all the animals that had been trapped in the center flying past us to safety.

As they passed us we could all feel the gratitude they extended to us for saving their lives. For a moment I almost forgot that we weren't done. I wanted to stand there and feel the love forever. But we had to move. We knew what was coming.

What we did next was the most dangerous thing we could think of doing, and we were doing it on purpose. We turned off our shields. We didn't want Abbadon to see what we had planned. But that meant we had only our earmuffs to protect us, and the shrieking had become even louder.

We had only a few moments before we would not be able to move. We threw our shields up over our backs as we ran back through the line of Shrieks dodging the animals running in the same direction, running as low as we could, hiding beneath our shields to be as invisible as possible.

The Shrieks we had stunned were still frozen as we made our way back through the line. As we ran, we could hear the roar of the coming storm. The Shrieks must have heard it too because the shrieking increased as they began moving through the woods trying to outrun the storm.

We watched them go, grateful that they were not coming towards us. But if the Shrieks made it to safety, wherever that was for them, before the storm arrived, we would have to face them again.

And then the wall of water arrived. It literally looked like a wall. It was taller than the trees and black as night. The wall cascaded over them, moving across the line like a car wash. If the Shrieks could feel anything, it must have been shocking to discover that it wasn't just water that drenched them. It was highly concentrated salt water.

Ariel was behind the wall of water pushing it away from the fleeing animals and us and into the lines of Shrieks. Once we were past the last line of paralyzed Shrieks, we turned and watched as the fleeing Shrieks first began to expand and then burst and dissolve. Within minutes the forest floor was littered with green blobs.

We knew what came next—the army of insects. We raced to the nearest tree and grabbed the lowest branch and pulled ourselves up. This time I knew that the tree had lowered its limbs for us. It wasn't an illusion, They moved. There wasn't time to contemplate what that might mean, because we could hear the skittering of insect legs and flying ahead of them the Priscillas looking triumphant.

The Priscillas all landed on my shoulders at the same time, and the two younger sisters kissed me on each cheek. Pris was still acting miffed, but I could tell from the gleam in her eyes that she was teasing me. It was good to have her back on my side.

"I was never not on your side, Missy," Pris said. "It was you acting as if we weren't to be trusted."

"I was wrong," I whispered.

"Could you say that a little louder, please?" Pris demanded.

"I was wrong," I said loud enough that almost everyone heard me and started to laugh.

"Imagine that!" Zeid said. I glowered at him, even though I knew that he too was teasing. Although I was exhausted, I was feeling good. We had defeated those Shrieks. We could defeat others. Or Earl and Ariel could. We had discovered that they didn't need us to stop the Shrieks anymore. They could do it without us.

But that left the bigger problem. Shatterskin. He didn't need the Shrieks to continue to shatter his way across the land. All they had been to him was a way to neutralize anyone who might be able to fight him. And if he thought it was important to do that, it meant there was a way to defeat him.

The next phase of our plan had to be put in place, and it would mean that I could no longer hide from being myself, or using the magic that I now knew that I had.

After the insects passed, we scrambled down from the trees and back to where we knew the circles would take us down to where Pita and Teddy would be waiting, ready to put our next plan into action.

Shatterskin thought he was coming to us, but we were going to him instead. But first, we needed to regroup, and prepare.

Fifty-Two

Besides Teddy and Pita, James and his men were waiting for us in the transport room. He was leaning on his brother, but otherwise looked unharmed. I rushed over and grabbed his hands. His daughter would never forgive me if something happened to him.

"You had me so scared, James," I said. And then to my complete embarrassment started to sob. James let go of his brother, John, and put his arms around me, holding me close without saying anything.

That made me cry even more. At that moment I realized how much I missed my Earth family and their constant care and attention. My mother was always hugging me, and I would shake it off thinking I was too old to be cuddled. Now I would give anything to be embraced by her again.

"I was terrified," I whispered to James, keeping my face buried in his coat.

James lifted my chin so I could see him. "So was I, Hannah. And yet, you did what you needed to do, and it worked."

"But what if one of you had been killed?"

"We weren't. And if that happens, Hannah, it won't be your fault. It's the kind of thing that happens. But you of all people know that what is called death is just one door closing while another opens."

"It won't make it hurt less for those of us who would miss you, though."

"No. It probably won't. But it will give you a sense of peace knowing that life transforms itself into other forms."

"Like the trees."

"Exactly like the trees, Hannah."

"You're calling me Hannah."

James smiled down at me and said, "You'll always be partly Hannah. That's a good thing. Think about what you learned during your time in the Earth Realm. That learning will always give you insights that some of us might not have since we haven't learned from that world. You have an expanded awareness that you will bring to everything if you remain open to it.

"Besides, Hannah, we all know you miss your Earth family and friends. That's only natural. Plus, you have had to grow from a young girl to a young woman in just a few months with the weight of a world on your shoulders. We've asked a lot of you."

James pulled a tissue from his jacket pocket and handed it to me.

"Thank you," I said, smiling through the tears running down my face. "And I hope when this is over I can come to stay with you and Liza and just be Hannah and not Kara Beth."

James smiled and said, "You can consider us your non-royal friends forever. Our village will always be a refuge for you."

"Well, I guess we better get ready to save it then," I sniffed.

"That we better," James answered while putting his arm around my shoulder. I wasn't sure if it was that he still needed to be supported after his brush with the stunning effect of the

Shrieks, or if it was me that needed to feel his arm around me.

Either way, I was as happy as I had been for quite a while. James made me feel like I was his daughter, and that was a feeling I was going to treasure forever.

As we turned to leave, I realized that the transport room was empty except for James and me. I was grateful that everyone had let me have my breakdown in private.

Teddy was waiting outside the door. "Hello, pumpkin toes," he said to me, taking my hand. James and I laughed so hard I was crying again. Once I got my breath, I turned to Teddy and hugged him too.

It was like hugging a furry rug, not quite the same as embracing James, but it felt great to be wrapped up in those big strong arms.

"Okay, you two. I think I am recovered enough to be ready for the next plan," I said.

"Not yet," Pris said flying towards me. "First, shower, clean clothes, and then we are all meeting in the planning room. Niko said you have an hour."

I said goodbye to James and Teddy and followed Pris down the hall to my room. As I walked, I tried to ground myself in the energy of the trees that held the rooms together.

"Take off your shoes," sounded in my head. Not a voice, a feeling of a voice.

I stopped and waited. Pris turned.

"Got something going on?" she asked.

When I nodded yes, she said, "Well, do it then."

"So you heard that?"

"Hum … not the same as you, but I know when the trees speak."

"It was the trees?"

"Well, who else would it be?" Pris said waving her arms

around her. We were surrounded by the soft lights generated by the roots that wove through the walls holding the earth in place.

"Well, yes, that too," she said to who knows who.

"And who are you talking to?"

Pris gave me one of her famous looks that implied I was a stone cold idiot.

"The trees!"

"And what did you mean by the 'well, that too,' remark then," I countered, almost as huffily as Pris.

Then we both laughed. We were two primadonnas doing a standoff. I could almost hear the trees chuckling.

"Well. Take your shoes off then," Pris said, settling herself on a root in the wall.

I did. I slid off my shoes and socks and felt the ground. It thrummed. I stood still, the light dimmed, I closed my eyes, calmed my breath, trying to feel the breath of the trees. And I waited.

It didn't take long. Within a few minutes, I knew what needed to be done next.

Fifty-Three

After a quick shower, and gratefully putting on the clean clothes lying on my bed, I was in the planning room with everyone else just under the hour time limit set by Niko.

Food was set out on the tables lining the walls. As always, it was a buffet filled with food that met all our individual needs. I promised myself that after all this was over, I would do something for all the invisible people who were providing for us.

I wasn't really hungry, but I knew that it was necessary to eat, so I filled my plate and joined everyone at the table.

Niko began, "Well, now we know that we didn't have to paralyze the Shrieks to drop the salt water on them after all. That means we can attack them without putting all of you in danger by being too close to them. It also means that we can stop the supply line to Shatterskin."

"Does that mean that we will only be dealing with the power left in Shatterskin?" John asked.

"That's what we believe," Niko answered. "However, we don't know how long that will be, or how quickly Abbadon can, or will, send replacement minions to bring the fresh batteries.

"The good news is that Lady and her crown of pileated dragons believe they have located the manufacturing plant where Abbadon makes the Shrieks. If we can destroy that plant, we can stop the Shrieks forever."

"We hope you have a plan to do that, Niko," John said. "I admit, your plans to stop the Shrieks worked perfectly, although I reserve judgment about the residual effects of the salt. However, no one has talked at all about the biggest danger."

Niko motioned for John to continue.

"When Shatterskin comes through, no one lives. He destroys so thoroughly it will take centuries before the ground recovers—if it ever does. Now your reports tell us that he is moving faster than ever and our earmuffs and shields are not going to protect us from him."

That was John. Questioning. Not quite on board. But we needed people to do that, otherwise we might stumble into something we would never get out of without some of us dying.

The Priscillas flew off my coat and arranged themselves on the edge of the table to look at me. I tried to shoo them away, but they stuck themselves there. Staring. Waiting.

Niko laughed. "Well, I see that the Priscillas know what is going to happen next." He turned to me and said, "Well, Kara Beth, are you going to tell us the plan?"

Zounds, I was hoping to gain more time, stall a little. But it seemed that wasn't going to happen. Although I did my best to fidget around a bit, hoping that what I was going to say would improve with a few more seconds of reprieve.

Everyone was looking at me. As I looked back at our team, I expected to see everyone looking at me with complete dismay, probably figuring that if I had a plan, it was going to fail. Couldn't blame them there. But I was surprised to see that there were a variety of looks.

Besides the Priscillas, both Niko and Aki had that look of anticipation as if they knew what I was going to do, and they approved. Sometimes they scared me with what they knew.

Others looked at me with pride.

Surprisingly Ruta was in that category, along with Beru, Teddy, Pita, and Zeid.

Zeid had a different kind of pride in his look though. I knew that once this was all over, I would have to address what was between us. But it would have to wait. I had no room for thinking about that right now.

Finally, the men from the village. James had the look of a father whose daughter was growing up; John was angry; and Kit, Mark, and Thomas were patiently waiting for my answer before passing judgment.

However, before I could speak, I was saved. I was pretty sure that Suzanne and Earl's entrance was timed perfectly for just that reason. Trying not to give away my total panic, I projected a "thank you" into their minds and in return received a feeling of warmth and safety. I wasn't alone.

"I'll be helping too, Kara," Link said.

I included him in my thanks and then settled back to let Earl and Suzanne run the show, at least for the moment.

Although he was up above in the woods, I could feel Cahir's presence so strongly at my side it felt as if I could reach out and pat him on his head. I almost laughed out loud when Cahir growled and snapped at my fingers reminding me that my time was coming soon.

"Get ready," Cahir said.

Well, I knew that's what he said even though it was just a feeling, like feeling the trees talking to me.

Thankfully, everyone had turned their attention to Earl. He didn't need to ask for it. Now that we had all seen his power as Coro, the man standing before us was even more majestic and commanding.

He took his time, looking at each person around the table for a long time. Perhaps he was taking a measure of who they were. The effects of his gaze resting on them was different for each person.

The doubters seemed to squirm a little more, and the ones who had looked at me with pride or acceptance looked more grounded and relaxed.

I prepared myself for his gaze resting on me, but it didn't. He looked at each Priscilla, made them giggle, and then passed right over me and took in the entire table.

I tried not to worry about why he had skipped me. Did he know that I wasn't up to what I was supposed to do next and he didn't want anyone to see my reaction when he looked at me?

There wasn't time for me to drag myself down too far because Earl started speaking. His voice filled every crevice of the room with power, assurance, and courage.

"Thank you for your bravery out there today," he began. "Yes, now we know how to eliminate the Shrieks, and I have sent small storms over every band of Shrieks that managed to escape. The insects have taken care of the remainders of the Shrieks that fled. We are attacking the supply lines as we speak.

"The trees have assured me that they can handle the amount of salt we have dumped. And once this is over, we'll help by sending clean rain down to wash the salt further down where the roots can do their work gathering it, using what's needed, and sending the rest back to the ocean.

"Too bad we didn't know earlier how easy this was going to be. But that's often the way.

"Things seem impossible, and then a few brave people of all races and creeds band together and find the solution. In this case, it's everyone around this table and all the ones who have supported all of you behind the scenes.

"We think that the solution to stopping Shatterskin will follow the same scenario. The solution is easy, but it will take bravery to carry it out."

That's when he turned to me and said, "Time to take over, Princess Kara Beth."

My heart froze. It was time. I was not ready. At all.

Fifty-Four

A long silence dragged out, and the longer it dragged out, the harder it got to speak. When I finally managed to squeak out a few words it was such a far cry from Earl's booming voice which inspired so much confidence that I was sure everyone in the room would burst out laughing.

When no one did, I straightened up and thought about all the people that were counting on me. Every moment I stalled, Shatterskin was busy destroying. If my plan worked, we wouldn't have to wait until his battery ran down, if it ever did. We could stop him now.

But first I had to tell a story. I looked to Ruta and Suzanne for support, and they both nodded at me to go on. It was my story to tell. I had to share what happened when Aki took me to the Oracle.

I don't know what I expected, but I was still trying to make sense of what happened. Ruta was part of the story. Grumpy Ruta who had treated me with disdain when I first arrived. Ruta, who had done his job only because Earl had told him to. Now I knew it was Earl's voice that moved through the wind that day in the clearing and told him to take care of me.

And Ruta had done his job of taking care of me, even

though it didn't seem like something he wanted to do. Over the past few months, Ruta didn't become less grumpy, but some of his disdain seemed to have faded.

It was always Ruta and Beru who made sure that everything I needed was always available. They were my protectors. Beru and I had developed a comfortable relationship, even though she sometimes treated me like an errant child, probably because I was. However, Ruta had stayed distant and just done his job.

Until the Oracle.

For me, the word oracle meant some mystical person or being who knew everything and only shed their wisdom on some people and always in riddles. That's what I expected. In a way, that's what I got.

After the hobbit door closed behind me, I couldn't see anything at all except for a small blue light. I felt my way around the walls until I was in front of it. By then my night vision had clicked on a bit, and I could see that the blue light was inside what looked like a tree trunk.

Since the walls were composed of tree roots, in one way a tree trunk was not surprising. However, we were at least fifty feet underground. How was there a tree trunk down here?

The blue light sparked, and I heard the question inside my head, "Is that your question for the Oracle? How is a tree trunk down below?"

"I guess it depends on how many questions I can have answered while I am here," I answered. "I would like to know, but that's not the most important question I have to ask. Anyway, if you are wise and all-knowing don't you know the question I am here to ask?"

I heard what sounded like chimes and decided it might be the Oracle laughing since the light had fluttered while it laughed.

"Ruta shared stories about you with me," she said. "He said you were a bit feisty. Of course, I know that you have always been that way."

At least I assumed it was a she, since the Oracle had a lovely lilting voice, and weren't most Oracles female? I didn't want to ask that question, though, because, once again, I didn't know how many questions she would answer.

But I couldn't help myself when I asked, "Ruta? You know Ruta? Do you speak with Ruta? And you know that I always have been feisty? Do I know you?"

If the Oracle had answered the question, I never heard it. Instead, the next thing I knew I was back in my bed, and it was morning, and Aki was sleeping in the air beside my bed.

It was Aki who showed me what had happened when I visited the Oracle. It was Ruta who told me who she was, but I didn't share that knowledge with the group. It was still too new for me. Afterward, if all went well, I could talk about it.

I told the group around the table that I had been practicing, and I thought I was ready to demonstrate but not in the closed room. I stood and said, "Follow me."

It was an odd feeling to have all those people following me. Even though I hadn't seen myself in a mirror for a long time, I knew that I was average everything: average height and unspectacular brown hair that I tied back in a ponytail.

And even though Zeid seemed to think I was beautiful, I am not. Just average. Although I have been told that my blue eyes sometimes do sparkle a bit. I was just a teenage girl leading a group of grownups to their destiny. Nothing to stress out about. I felt Cahir's presence and his reminder that I wasn't alone and felt a little better.

A few minutes later we were in our practice room. The last time we were there I was trying to send practice blasts with my shield to a target without hurting anyone. This time the target was a massive piece of metal at the end of the room.

"Would you all stand behind me please," I asked and turned to face them. Then without saying anything, I sprung into the air, spun around and headed for the target, shooting lightning from my hands.

Within seconds the entire piece of metal was melted and lying on the ground.

I landed as gracefully as possible. In practice, I kept falling over, but miraculously I remained standing this time and turned to look at everyone in the back of the room trying to look as if what I did was an everyday occurrence, not something that Aki and I had been working on ever since the Oracle.

On the way to the meeting, I had felt the trees' energy pulsing through me opening more of my memory of how to access the power within me to fly and to produce that lightening.

James was smiling at me. His brother and the other men from Beru's village stood open mouthed staring at what I had done.

Everyone else looked as if they had expected it. "Well, that's a relief," Niko said. "You were cutting that close." Seeing my puzzled face, he added. "Yes, we knew you could do that, it's one reason we needed you back in Erda."

Niko turned to Aki and asked, "Is it enough?"

Aki looked at me and whispered, "It's best to tell the whole truth here, Kara Beth."

I knew she was right, so I answered. "I'm not sure. We've been practicing, and I am better than I was a few days ago, or even this morning. But we can't wait to find out. The Riff is only a few miles away from another village.

"I am going to need everyone's help to do this, that is if you are willing. I'll understand if you don't trust me enough.

"However, I don't think we can do it without everyone. All I can promise you is that I will do everything not to let you down, and to destroy Shatterskin before he gets to that village."

Zeid stepped forward. "I'm ready. When do we go?"

"Now," I said. "I have assignments for each of you. Then we go."

Everyone stepped forward, and tears rushed to my eyes in gratitude and love for every one of them. Tears might not be expected for a leader, but it was my way.

I looked down to my left wrist at the two bracelets that sat there. My friendship bracelet from Johnny, and the one with the jasper stone given to me by Professor Link.

One was my past, and one was my future. Seeing them both there reminded me that I was of both worlds and that was what made me stronger than Abbadon's Shatterskin. And I was going to prove it.

Fifty-Five

Thirty minutes later some of us were above ground and moving towards Shatterskin. Teddy and his team had tweaked our ear muffs again. We needed even more protection from the sonic booms that Shatterskin was sending out. Working against the Shrieks had helped perfect that part of our protection. We planned to stop Shatterskin before he stopped us—well killed us—but we had to get close enough to do it. Getting close enough was one part of the problem.

The other part was that our entire plan rode on the belief that if we sent enough heat and energy towards Shatterskin, he would melt the same way I had melted the metal down below. When I had explained that was our plan there had been complete silence until John spoke up. "Seriously, you are going to melt Shatterskin. Are you crazy?"

"Probably, but I've been told that it will work," was my answer.

I didn't tell them who told me, but they thought it was the Oracle and I wasn't going to say otherwise. I agreed with them that on the one hand, it sounded too simple to be true that all we had to do was melt him.

But, on the other side, it wasn't simple at all. We had to get close enough to blast him, without him killing us first. Not a simple feat. In fact, it seemed impossible. Shatterskin could shatter trees and rocks. Our bodies would not be able to sustain a hit from his sonic blasts.

All our earmuffs were doing was lowering the decibel level of the sound, but even what we didn't hear could kill us. So we needed to be where he didn't expect us.

Which meant our first plan was to make him think we were someplace we weren't. To do that, we turned on our shields. We didn't believe that our reflecting Shatterskin's sounds back to him would hurt him. All we wanted was Abbadon to send Shatterskin after us.

As soon as our shields started reflecting, Shatterskin turned our way. The sonic sounds and the horrible noise of the trees as they were ripped from the earth was terrifying. It was hard not to break down watching the death of everything in Shatterskin's path that couldn't get out of his way.

Cahir had evacuated everything that could move far from what was going on, for which we were grateful. The Ginetes and Whistle Pigs were deeper underground hoping to get behind Shatterskin before he collapsed the tunnels where we had just spent the last few days. They were also busy preparing Shatterskin's final surprise.

The rest of us were above ground. Really above ground. But not behind our shields. We were flying. Not the way I had flown underground. I could not sustain that kind of flying for long, and we had a long way to go. Instead, all of us were riding the pileated dragons.

Riding the dragons was almost as terrifying as watching the destruction on the ground. We were flying as high as we could over Shatterskin's head, hoping that he couldn't see us. Below us, we could see the ripping of the earth and trees as Shatterskin passed. Even as high as we were, we could feel the vibrations from the thunderous noise it made. We had to get behind him before he noticed that we were not where we had attached our shields to the trees.

Suzanne had given us each a harness that we placed over our dragon. The harness was not for the dragon. They knew how to fly us to where we were going. They were for us. I knew I was not the only one terrified of flying on a dragon. No one had done it before. What if we fell off, or froze to death? It was so cold I was shivering within minutes. Or maybe I was trembling from fear.

I could see Ruta and Beru riding together on one of the larger dragons. Beru was holding onto Ruta for dear life. I wasn't sure which one was more terrified. They both hated heights. Ruta especially. But Ruta had to be there. He had a task to do that only he could do.

I was riding Lady. I knew we were asking a lot of the dragons. We were heavy. They weren't used to flying with a passenger, but it was the only way to get where we were going fast enough.

I had asked about the Sound Bubble, and Suzanne had looked at me as if I was crazy. "You and that bubble. We'll ride it again, but for this, it won't work. It would shatter, and it can't get high enough. One blast from Shatterskin and that would be the end."

All of us were tuned into Link's channel, and no one was to do anything until everyone was in place. After what seemed like an eternity, everyone checked in and said they were ready.

Massive dust clouds were rising from the ground, whipped up by Ariel's wind. The dust obscured our view of the land, but it also obscured Shatterskin's view of what was going on above his head, and behind him.

We were wearing goggles. The dragons were not, but they had assured us, through Lady, that they would be okay.

"Now," Link said, and Lady and I began our descent.

It was now or never. As we dove straight down through the dust, the noise level increasing, I touched the star around my neck and saw what I was looking for: Shatterskin's Achilles heel.

"Go," I shouted to myself, and jumped.

Fifty-Six

Lady had gotten me close enough to fly to the opening behind Shatterskin's neck. We knew there had to be an opening because the Shrieks had been seen swarming over Shatterskin every time they brought him a new battery. It seemed obvious that they didn't need all those Shrieks for that job, so we figured that they were hiding how they got inside of the machine. They were protecting Shatterskin's Achilles heel.

My plan was not to kill Shatterskin from the outside, but from the inside. It was something he would not be expecting. Actually, we didn't believe Shatterskin was thinking. We were sure that Abbadon controlled Shatterskin somehow, and the answer lay inside of that metal skin.

All I needed to do was find the hole and fly inside without dying on the way—no big deal. The perspective that the star had given me revealed the opening, and I thought that once inside we had a great chance of stopping him.

The plan was to melt the battery and whatever else was driving him, and then deal with Shatterskin's body when it was still and silent. At the very least, I hoped to stop him from making any sounds. If we could prevent him from moving, that was even better, because the Ginete and Whistle Pigs needed me to stop him as close to where they were going as possible, since he would be hard to move as dead weight.

As I headed towards the opening at breakneck speed, I was happy that everyone else was as safely out of range as possible. They were either high up with the dragons heading to another destination, or far below building the final trap.

My flight from Lady to Shatterskin was the longest few seconds of my life. I knew if I didn't hit the opening on target I would die. I only hoped that I would die before I shattered apart into a million pieces. A split second away from the door, I fired a beam of lightning at it to melt the covering and make the opening big enough for me to pass through.

There was a mind-blowing moment of fear hoping that it would work before I hit the hole and slid in. I could feel the edge of the hot metal rip along my left arm, but the pain only helped me focus.

We had thought that once inside Shatterskin we wouldn't be affected by the sound. We reasoned that he had to have some system that blocked his own weapon from shattering his insides. Luckily we were right. The only sound I could hear was coming through the opening that I had made when I blasted the covering off of the entrance to Shatterskin's insides.

I hovered inside using my new found flying ability, and a second later, the Priscillas flew in through the open hole, each of them holding a small shield Teddy had made for them. They had waited until the door was open before leaving Lady and following me, using their shields to block as much sound as possible.

For them, with their tiny bodies, this was almost a suicide mission, but I couldn't persuade them not to come. I was never so happy to see anyone. But we didn't have time to celebrate. We had only just begun.

I took their shields and welded them in place with the energy from my hands to block as much outside sound as possible. Once I closed the opening, my job was to find the battery and melt it. The Priscillas were to pull cables and cut wires wherever they saw them.

Inside Shatterskin it was pitch black, and although relatively quiet, he was always moving, and we had to stay suspended in the air to keep from being banged against the walls.

My backpack contained balls of tree pitch collected by Ruta for me. I stuck them to the metal and then lit them hoping they would stay. But if not, at least they would fall inside of Shatterskin and maybe do some damage.

Once we had enough light, I could see what looked like the battery and headed towards it, blasting it as I went.

Two things happened that scared the ziffer out of me. One, I tried to talk to Link and the team and let them know where we were and realized that I couldn't hear them. Which meant they couldn't hear me either. And two, Shatterskin starting shaking himself, throwing the Priscillas and me against the walls.

I yelled to the Priscillas to grab onto me, and we descended together holding on to a cable that led to the battery. Pris shouted in my ear, "He must know we are inside, so make it quick."

As if I didn't know. The tree sap started giving out, and I stuck more on the walls and lit them with a blast of energy. Some stuck, others didn't, but the light they gave off made it easier to keep my eyes on the target. I did my best to avoid the things that were shaking loose inside of Shatterskin. I wondered if he knew what he was doing or if it was the machine's version of a death rattle.

I knew that even after I melted the battery, we were still in trouble. Because our communication was down, we couldn't coordinate our plans. I couldn't believe how much I missed everyone's voice in my head. I had thought it was annoying, but I would have given anything now to hear something.

We were on our own. The problem was, once we stopped Shatterskin, the rest of the team would begin their attack thinking that we were safely away.

"Well then we better be safely away," Pris said, reading my mind. Thankfully we could still hear each other even though Pris kept insisting on actually yelling at me.

I knew what she was doing. She was making me angry. Angry worked. The Priscillas tucked into my jacket to be safe as I blasted everything I had at the battery. The shaking stopped and the Priscillas flew off to cut wires because we could still hear faint booming sounds.

We had stopped him from moving, but not blasting sonic booms. There had to be an extra battery. I stuck pitch balls everywhere to light our way. We cut wires and melted anything that looked as if it contained power, but we could still hear the booms.

La called, "Up here!"

We all looked up to see her at the top of Shatterskin's head pointing at a black box behind his eyes. Ah. The brain. Time to blast it to kingdom come. "Get back," I yelled, and flew at the box blasting it with every bit of energy that I had. I let the anger fuel me. The view from the star had begun to fade, and I knew I was drawing my last bit of reserves.

It had to be enough.

Fifty-Seven

"You'll have to help," I signaled to the Priscillas when I realized that the box was still intact even after all the lightning I had directed at it. That seemed impossible, but the Priscillas joined me, and we sent every ounce of energy that we had to that little box. Nothing happened.

I was terrified out of my mind. After all this, we couldn't stop Shatterskin? No one would be able to get close enough to stop him unless we ended his sonic blasts. What if the box was made of something that could not be destroyed? Perhaps we had lost after all.

I thought of all the people of Erda counting on us to stop this monster. I thought of my family that had taught me about illusion. And I knew we had forgotten one crucial thing.

"Stop," I yelled. "It's done. I know it is. We destroyed that box. It only looks like it is still intact because Shatterskin is using the power we are sending him to block our view of what we have done and to produce his blasts. We have to withdraw everything from him now. The only power Shatterskin has right now is to produce an illusion, and we are feeding it."

Not doing anything while the sonic blasts continued, knowing that the sound was shattering everything in its path, was the hardest thing we had done yet. But Aki's training kicked in. We calmed ourselves. Pris hummed. We closed our eyes. I thought about the power of Love and how it had saved my family and me in the Earth Realm time and again.

Then the Priscillas and I were at peace. And the noise stopped. It had worked. Opening our eyes, we could see that the box had been destroyed, and it was only the illusion that had kept us from seeing that our blasts had dissolved it.

In the back of my mind, I realized that Abbadon was much cleverer than I had thought. But I tabled that thought. We didn't have time to deal with it right at that moment.

The rest of the team would be beginning our final part of the plan, and we had to get out before it started, and there was no way to tell anyone that we were still inside.

After so much noise and movement, when Shatterskin came to a stop, and the booms had ceased, the silence was deafening. There was still a little light left from the pitch balls, but it was fading, and the four of us didn't have any energy left to relight them.

We should have been happy about the stillness and silence, but we knew that meant that Pita and Teddy's teams would now be doing their part of the attack. Well, it wasn't an attack as much as it was a removal.

Until we were trapped inside of Shatterskin, I had thought it was a great plan. Now it looked like we would be removed along with him. Shatterskin began to lurch, and the four of us screamed. Any other time I might have laughed at the squeak the fairies made when they screamed. My scream wasn't much better. Not enough energy to give a good yell.

We screamed, not because Shatterskin had come alive again, but because we knew that the ground beneath him had opened and he had begun to sink. I was proud of Teddy and Pita. Their plan was working. While we had been busy shutting Shatterskin down, multiple teams of Ginete and Whistle pigs had been frantically digging.

The trees were helping of course by lining the walls of a hole big enough to drop Shatterskin into. But they had to wait until we shut off the movement and the sound to finish it.

With a silent and still Shatterskin, they would tunnel to the surface and open a circle beneath him. Shatterskin would then slip beneath the surface and would end up deep in the earth.

Eventually, Shatterskin would sink low enough to end up in a molten lava flow that the Whistle Pigs were directing his way. He would be gone forever. But then, if we didn't get out, we would be gone forever too.

"I have a plan," I tried to tell the Priscillas, but the words stuck in my throat.

That's when I realized that we were running out of air. The pitch balls were consuming the last of the oxygen.

Pris answered me inside my head. "We heard you, so what is it?" In my mind's eye, I pictured the plan and hoped the three of them understood. They nodded. We had one chance.

We each grabbed a burning ball of pitch and flung it through one of Shatterskin's eyes. I could only use my right hand. My left arm had stopped working. It had also stopped hurting which didn't seem like a good sign.

All four of us screamed as the balls burned our hands, but we managed to get them to fly together at Shatterskin's right eye burning a tiny hole in it.

A small amount of air rushed in, and we each took a deep breath and then helped La, the smallest of the fairies to scramble through the hole. Then we waited. Either someone was out there or not. But at least La would survive, and Shatterskin had been stopped.

I gathered Pris and Cil in my arms and found a wire for us to sit on, and then I passed out. My last thoughts were that I would never get to tell Zeid that I remembered him and that I would never be Queen of Erda.

Fifty-Eight

"Why didn't you use the safety button Teddy gave you," Beru asked.

A few days had passed since I had awoken back in my old room at the Castle. When I had first opened my eyes, I was astonished to find myself in my own bed with Beru sitting beside me holding my hand.

"Shh," she had said, "Go back to sleep." And I had. Off and on for days, and with only Beru there to take care of me, I knew that meant there was something terribly wrong. Where was everyone else?

I tried to ask, but when Beru didn't answer, I followed her instructions to go back to sleep. I had decided that for the time being it was best not to know what had happened to my friends because I knew if they were safe they would be there with me.

When Beru finally asked me a question I knew she was ready to answer mine.

I figured that I was better because she had helped me sit at a small table at the foot of the bed. The metal toadstools had appeared with food, and I had to restrain myself from patting their heads I was so happy to see them.

"Well," Beru demanded again. "Why didn't you use it?"

"If I tell you, will you tell me where everyone is even if it is terrible news? I am imagining the worst, and it would be better to stop imagining and just know."

Beru didn't answer me, just sat there with her arms crossed, frowning at me.

"Because," I said, and then stopped.

"Because, what?"

"I didn't know if that meant I could take Pris and Cil with me. I couldn't leave them there. Makes me a foolish person I know, because obviously, I should have tried it."

I started to sob. I had been trying not to break down from the moment I had woken up the first time. Finally, I couldn't keep it in anymore.

"What are you crying about?" Beru asked.

I answered Beru in the most snarky voice I had ever used. I didn't care anymore. I had already hurt everyone else. "I lived, but no one else did? What was the point of doing any of this?"

Beru sighed. "Kara Beth, perhaps before you make up your mind that you did the wrong thing, you might want to hear a story."

"Sure, go ahead, tell me one, but I doubt it is going to make me feel better."

I drank whatever strange drink the metal toadstool had put in front of me and staggered back to bed. My left arm was wrapped in a bandage from my shoulder to my wrist, but it worked, and I found a sliver of gratitude for that.

Lying back against the pillow, I closed my eyes and waited, prepared to fall into a depression and never come out again.

****

As Beru began to speak, I waited for her to tell me everyone had died. Instead, she told me the story about what had happened to the rest of the team.

"After you dived through that hole in Shatterskin, we waited for Lady to come with us, but she insisted on circling above to wait for you. It turns out, that was a wise decision, but that's the end of the story, so I'll get back to it.

"The rest of us flew on to the plant where we knew Abbadon was making the Shrieks. As you know, Earl, Ariel, and the Priscillas' insects had destroyed every visible Shriek, but we knew there were more inside the factory.

"However, we believed that it was not just Shrieks inside that building. We thought that Abbadon was using villagers to make the Shrieks, so we couldn't just destroy the building. We planned to stun the remaining Shrieks the same way we had in the woods, rescue whoever was inside, and then let Coro and his storm destroy it.

"It was a good plan. Except what we discovered inside was so much worse than we thought it would be."

By then, I was sitting up in bed anxious to hear what had happened.

"So you made it into the wasteland safely?"

"We did. But the ground around the building was so shattered it made it difficult to get inside without falling into one of the crevices. The building itself was levitated a few feet off the ground, so Aki had to help all of us who don't know how to levitate up into the building. Thankfully we were invisible behind our shields, and inside the building there was no shrieking. Most likely so the beings inside wouldn't die from the Shrieks. Instead, they were dying from something else."

When Beru saw me start to ask another question she said, "Let me tell it my way, please? I need to tell the whole story, because maybe then I can begin to forget it."

I nodded, but my fists were clutching the sheets, and I felt as if the breath in my body was clogged up inside my chest.

"It was a huge, open space, like an Earth factory. At the end of what resembled an assembly line, a Shriek would pop out and then slither over to another room where they waited. Maybe to be called into action. Or they had to dry out or something before they worked. For whatever reason, we could see that it would be fairly easy to kill them off if we could stop the machines."

Beru held up her hand reminding me not to ask questions. "I know. Just turn them off. But we didn't know how because the machines were not run by energy from the trees, or nature. Remember there weren't any trees or nature, the Shrieks and Shatterskin had killed all the life they could find.

"Abbadon needed another form of energy. We suspected what that source was when we realized that when Shatterskin destroyed villages, we rarely found the bodies of the villagers. We had a suspicion he was using them to run the machines. We were partially right and partially wrong. They weren't running the machines the way you might expect.

"Instead, there were hundreds of beings hooked up to the devices on the assembly line, unable to move. It was their life essence that was running the machines. Abbadon was draining them, one at a time, to build the monsters that destroyed their land and killed their loved ones.

"It was the most horrific thing we had ever seen, and I know that I will never be able to forget it. The beings stared at us with unseeing eyes, and the only way we could tell that they were still alive was they were still hooked up to the machines.

"The floor was littered with dead bodies that had been unhooked once their life force was gone. How could we shut off the machines, Hannah, if we didn't know what would happen to those poor beings?

"Someone had to decide what to do. Someone had to take responsibility because we didn't know how long it would be until the newly made Shrieks in the other room would awaken."

"Who did?" I whispered and then realized that I already knew the answer.

I took Beru's hand, and we cried together.

Fifty-Nine

"It killed some of them. Right then. We could see it. The last of their life force drained out, and they were gone."

I pulled myself closer to Beru and hugged her. "It had to be done, Beru. You couldn't rescue them with the machines on. But I'm sorry."

We stayed that way for a long moment, then Beru pulled away, wiping her eyes, although the tears still ran down her cheeks at the memory.

"We had no idea we would find so many beings there. They were from all different villages. But they were barely alive and couldn't help us rescue them. We figured out how to unhook them from the machines, and once we did that we took the ones that were still living and brought them outside to the dragons.

"Niko had alerted Professor Link as soon as we had stepped into the building and he had sent more dragons to transport the bodies."

Beru's face brightened at the memory. "You wouldn't have believed it, Kara. There were hundreds of them waiting there, watching the way that they do, cocking their heads back and forth. We had no idea that there were that many pileated dragons in Erda. At the most, we thought maybe besides Lady there were ten more like her, but not hundreds. It was beautiful to see. So much life. So different from what we saw all around us and inside that building.

"We found rope in the factory and did our best to tie one person on each dragon. As they flew away, we could see their wings flashing white and black, and the red on their heads was like a living beacon. The dragons were flying low as they could so that they wouldn't freeze their passengers. We prayed we were doing a good enough job roping their passengers on. "

Beru got up and went to the table and picked up one of the drinks the metal toadstools had left. She took a big swallow, paused, and slowly returned to the chair by the bed. I knew that whatever she was going to tell me next was not going to be good, and I steeled myself for the news. So far everything she had told me sounded like a horrible memory, but here she was. I reasoned that they must have succeeded. But when Beru looked at me with the saddest eyes I had ever seen, I was terrified all over again. Something terrible had happened. What was it?

"Something terrible did happen, Kara. We have been living with terrible things for so long I thought I could handle anything. However, the news we would hear was from far away. People in villages were dying. The land was being destroyed. Trees were shattered everywhere. Abbadon was living up to his name as the destroyer.

"We were used to that news. And even though some of us lost relatives who had lived nearer to Shatterskin's Riff, we hadn't seen it. However, at the plant, we were surrounded by shattered brown earth. There was no visible life anywhere except for us, the dragons, and the half-dead beings we were trying to rescue.

It was hard work, but we were getting it done. What we had forgotten was the room full of Shrieks. We could have dealt with them as soon as we got there. We could have taken the salt and water we had brought with us and sprinkled it over every one of them while they stood there immobile. But we didn't.

"The sight of those beings hooked up to the machines took all rational thought away. All we could think about was saving them, and we forgot the Shrieks."

I waited, holding my breath.

"They woke up and started Shrieking. Most of us had laid our shields down to make it easier to move people. Some of us had slipped the earmuffs off and had them hung around our necks, or had put them by the door to pick up on our way out. Niko and Aki were the only ones who had kept their shields on their back and their earmuffs on. It was a good thing because if they hadn't, we all would have died."

Beru ignored my gasp as I fell back against my pillow. She must mean some of them died. Who?

"At the first blast of the Shrieks, those of us who had our earmuffs around our necks got them on before it did too much damage.

"James was one of them. He grabbed all the earmuffs by the door and got one on his brother. But in the short time it took for him to get them on all the men, the damage had been done. Niko and Aki rushed the Shrieks and threw salt and water on them.

"They managed to stop the shrieking, but not before all the remaining beings we had not gotten onto the dragons yet had died. Even if we had ear muffs for them, the shrieking was too much in their weakened state.

"Most of the dragons had taken off with their passengers, and only a few were left on the ground when the shrieking started.

"All but one managed to lift off before they were too stunned to move. Once Niko and Aki stopped the Shrieks, the dragons returned, and we helped them tie the wounded dragon onto her sisters. I hope she survived."

"And the rest of the team?" Beru knew what I was asking. Did they live? Where were they? Did Ruta save them?"

This was the secret. Ruta was a healer. Ruta had asked me to keep it a secret after the Oracle had told me. I had agreed because we were afraid that there was a traitor in our midst, and Ruta would be targeted because of his healing abilities.

But now, it had to be known. Ruta would have arranged for the dragons to bring the wounded to him. We would deal with finding the traitor later.

Beru looked away, perhaps arranging her face. I prepared to hear the worst.

"Many of the people from the factory didn't make it. They were almost dead when we found them. Even Ruta couldn't save them."

I waited.

Beru gulped and whispered, "One of the men from my village didn't make it."

I couldn't ask, so I waited again.

"It was Kit."

"And that's it?"

Beru knew what I was asking. I felt grief for Kit, but also an overwhelming sense of relief flooded over me thinking of the people that were safe. As I started crying, I asked a question I had been reserving for last.

"And the Priscillas?"

"They have been helping Ruta. Everyone has been helping Ruta or resting from their injuries. You will see them tomorrow."

Seeing that I had dissolved into a hopeless pile of weeping, Beru rose to go. I wanted to shout with joy, but I had to ask the question that had been eating at me since I had woken up.

"One more question, Beru. Would the button have worked for all of us?"

"No. Only the person who was wearing it. You did the right thing, Kara Beth. You saved Pris and Cil.

"Now rest. It's a big day tomorrow."

Sixty

A week later, all of us were having dinner together in the Castle's atrium. I thought back to the first time I had dinner in the Castle with Beru, Ruta, Suzanne, and Earl. I had been so clueless. No wonder they called me "little one." I was a child. A child who had no memory of ever living in Erda.

Now I had memories I wished I could forget, and I was no longer a child. I couldn't afford to be anymore. Knowing where my thoughts were taking me, Suzanne reached over and squeezed my hand. I looked at her gratefully. Without her, I wouldn't have any connection to my past life in Earth. Even though I would probably never be able to return, I knew she would let them know how much I missed them and had treasured my time with my Earth family.

Just thinking about them brought tears to my eyes, especially thinking about Johnny. Suzanne and I had met privately before the dinner. She told me the portal was to be opened briefly and she was going to make a quick visit to the Earth dimension. Was there anything I needed her to say to my Earth family and friends while she was there?

Trying to be as brave as possible, I slipped my friendship bracelet off my wrist leaving only the bracelet from Professor

Link. I had to return the one from Earth and set Johnny free. Johnny needed to move on and not wait for me. What might have been would never be. Even if we destroyed Abbadon and I was able to visit the Earth Realm again, I could never live there, and Johnny could not live in Erda. He was needed in Earth, even more than he knew.

And then there was Zeid. Even though I hadn't seen him yet, I knew who he was now. Beru told me Zeid was taking care of some business with his family, but I knew he was waiting. Waiting until I had taken care of what I had to do. My arm felt empty without my friendship bracelet from Johnny, but it had to be done, for Johnny, for me, and for Zeid.

I brought my attention back to the room and the crowded table. Except for Zeid, everyone was there including Pita and his brothers, and Teddy. James and the remaining men from the village were there too, although now that they were rested they were returning to their village in the morning.

Even with all the joyful laughing and talking that was circling the table, there was an undercurrent of sadness. Kit had died. Everyone had scars. Lady's friend had also died. However, if it hadn't been for Ruta, there would have been so many more deaths.

"They would have wanted you to feel joyful, Kara Beth," Professor Link said.

This time Link was not in my head but sat on the other side of me. "You did well, young lady," he whispered, and I bowed my head so he wouldn't see how much his praise meant to me.

I knew he was right. We had to live and not slide into depression. No one who had lost their lives would want that for any of us. They had fought so all of us could be safe.

The Shrieks and Shatterskin were gone. Earl and Ariel had leveled the plant with the last remaining Shrieks inside. But

Abbadon still lived. Until he was stopped we were still in danger. We knew Abbadon must be planning something even if we didn't know what it was. He was not going to give up his desire to destroy just because we had killed his machines.

Looking around the table, I couldn't believe that one of the people sitting there could be a traitor. I prayed that it was a mistake. I knew everyone on our team, and until I knew otherwise, I would treat them as the treasures that I knew they were. If there was a traitor, they weren't sitting at the table. I was sure of it.

Earl held up his glass and yelled, "How about a toast?"

"Yeah!" we all yelled back and held up our glasses too. Even the metal toadstools raised their trays into the air.

"To this faithful, loyal, and brave community," Earl said, smiling at me. I smiled back and said, "So say we all." I loved this saying from one my favorite TV shows back in Earth. It was a response that I had taught everyone, so I wasn't surprised when they all responded, "So say we all."

Putting my glass down, I asked, "So, I know that most of you were brought to Ruta's Healing Center by the dragons. But how did the Priscillas and I get back here?"

The three fairies were taking turns sitting on my head, or at the table staring back up at me, and when all three of them turned to hear the answer, I knew they didn't know how we got home either.

Beru started to laugh and was joined by Suzanne.

"What's so funny?" I demanded.

"It was the Sound Bubble. After you helped La escape, she was able to contact Link who sent the bubble. I couldn't get you on my back since you were unconscious, so we all rode back in the bubble."

"I missed the bubble ride?" I said in a huff. "So that's what it takes to get in that thing. Almost die?"

"Not always, Princess."

We all turned to see Zeid standing in the doorway. My heart leaped, and I wanted to run to him, but it wasn't time.

A great "hurrah" rang out across the table as everyone jumped up to slap Zeid on the back or shake his hand.

There had to be a story here that no one had told me yet. But there was time for me to learn it. I had returned to Erda to stay.

Epilogue

A few weeks later…

Zeid and I stood with Niko, Aki, Beru, and Ruta on the hill looking down on a meadow that led into the village of Eiddwen. It was the meadow where I had played as a child, and the home our family would come back to when we were not at the Castle. It would be the first time I would see my father Darius since I had returned to Erda.

I knew he was ill. I had been told that was why he had not traveled to the Castle to greet me. I knew there were more reasons than that, but no one would tell me what they were. I knew that as always, they wanted me to discover it for myself.

Zeid and I were waiting for two old friends before heading down into the village to spend a few days to rest, and see my father before heading out on our next mission to stop Abbadon.

"I'm nervous," I said grabbing Zeid's hand. "I haven't seen them since we were all in Earth, and while we were there, I didn't know who we were."

"As you know, Kara, they didn't remember it either except as a dream. It took Leif almost a year of Earth time to regain all his memories."

"And that's when he stopped traveling to the Earth dimension?" I asked, even though I already knew the answer.

The people of Erda hadn't known that the three of us would not completely remember who we were as soon as we returned. Except for Sarah.

"Sarah remembered before she stepped into the portal, didn't she?"

"She did. That's why she didn't come with you. She was afraid she would hinder the return of your memory."

"I didn't even know she was in Erda until that day they sent me to the Oracle. Even though all I saw was the blue light, it felt like the woman I knew as Sarah."

Zeid laughed. "Yes, she wondered how quickly you would realize she was the Oracle in the tree."

"I still don't understand it though. Is Sarah an Oracle or not? And if she is an Oracle of some kind, then Leif is probably something more than just the man I remember from Earth."

When Zeid simply smiled at me, I knew he wasn't going to tell me. It was another thing for me to discover. But I could wait because right now I was getting a gift from my life in Earth.

I watched as the Sound Bubble descended a few yards away and the two people I knew as Leif and Sarah stepped out. Within seconds, I was running to greet them, ready to be gathered into their open arms. Whoever they were in Erda would wait. I had never been so happy to see anyone.

I trusted what I didn't know would be revealed and together we would fight Abbadon's new weapon.

For now, I planned to rejoice in being reunited with my friends. With the Priscillas riding in my pocket, we made our way down into the village and our next adventure together.

Love and magic made us strong. Above us, the sun shone through a crystal blue sky, and the trees bent in greeting as we passed. Life was beautiful, and we were going to keep it that way.

Author's Note

As I was writing the *Karass Chronicles*, I kept wondering what the other dimension was like that Suzanne, Leif, Sarah, Ariel, and Eric had gone to. What did they do there? What made it different from the Earth dimension?

Finding out about Erda was both exhilarating and slightly terrifying. I loved it when I would start writing and a world flowed out from my fingers that I had never seen or heard of before. But it was also scary because what if no one liked this world but me? What if it didn't make sense?

During our morning talks, I would ask Del things like, "How do you think I could kill a green blob or a big metal machine?" Just asking the questions usually prompted an idea, but unless I started writing about it, I remained stuck.

But that is what writing, or any creative project, is all about anyway, isn't it? We step out of the way, and magic happens. But we have to do the physical act of writing, or painting, or dancing, or planting a garden to experience it.

Halfway through Shatterskin, something wonderful happened. I started seeing myself in Erda. It became almost as real to me as the Earth dimension.

It is the planet Earth, or Gaia, after all. The same one we live on right now. But the people, the towns, the countryside, the choices, the fairies, dwarfs, Whistle Pigs—well, they look just a bit different here than there don't they?

Some little tidbits you might like:

When I was about three years old, I woke up one night and saw a gray wolf sitting by the bedroom door. He was sitting there as quiet as could be, but I thought it strange that a wolf was in my room. I remember tiptoeing into my parent's bedroom and telling them there was a wolf in my room. They said something like, "It's only a dream, honey, go back to sleep."

I returned to my bedroom, said goodnight to the wolf, and went back to sleep. Although I don't remember if I ever physically saw him after that (had I seen him?) I have often felt him near me. So I had to bring Cahir, my wolf, with me on this journey.

Beru and Ruta came from reading Beryl Markham's book, *West With The Night*. The names fit into the story perfectly, even though, of course, they are not elves or stump like creatures in her book. I just loved the names. *West With The Night* is fantastic by the way!

Lady is patterned after the pileated woodpecker that visits me—yes for real—at the feeder on my deck. There are two or three that visit, but Lady is the one that comes the most often. I watched her and wondered if in another dimension she might be a dragon. And so she is in Erda!

The trees. What can I say about trees. Trees have always spoken to me, and now I am married to a tree person, so tree books are loaded into both our Kindles. After reading Richard Powers' book, *The Overstory*, I was even more inspired to make trees, and nature, the key to the harmony of Erda, because we know that this is the truth after all.

And of course, you recognize the Cain and Abel story. As

for the snake spaceship with the brothers that caused it all, well, who says they didn't. It's all a story, isn't it?

In the next book, *Deadsweep*, Leif and Sarah from the *Karass Chronicles* play a more prominent role. Can you guess what Leif is in Erda?

If you would like to read a short prequel to both these series I'll send it to you for free.

It answers a few questions about the brothers who seeded Earth and Erda, and a little bit about where Suzanne really came from.

I'll tell you a secret: Earl and Ariel are not Suzanne's blood parents. And she has a sister Meg. More mystery. And another series, *The Chronicles of Thamon*.

Get this free short story here: becalewis.com/fantasy.

Love, Beca

PS To be the first to know when there are new books, please join my mailing list at BecaLewis.com.

Connect with me online:

Twitter: http://twitter.com/becalewis
Facebook: https://www.facebook.com/becalewiswriter
Pinterest: https://www.pinterest.com/theshift/
Instagram: http://instagram.com/becalewis
LinkedIn: https://linkedin.com/in/becalewis

OTHER BOOKS BY BECA

The Karass Chronicles - Paranormal Mystery

Karass

Pragma

Jatismar

Exousia

Stemma

Paragnosis

The Return To Erda Series - Fantasy

Shatterskin

Deadsweep

Abbadon

The Chronicles of Thamon - Fantasy

Anyone

Everyone

Allone

The Shift Series - Nonfiction

Living in Grace: The Shift to Spiritual Perception

The Daily Shift: Daily Lessons From Love To Money

The 4 Essential Questions: Choosing Spiritually Healthy Habits

The 28 Day Shift To Wealth: A Daily Prosperity Plan

The Intent Course: Say Yes To What Moves You

Perception Parables: - Fiction - very short stories

Love's Silent Sweet Secret: A Fable About Love

Golden Chains And Silver Cords: A Fable About Letting Go

Advice: - Nonfiction

A Woman's ABC's of Life: Lessons in Love, Life and Career from Those Who Learned The Hard Way

ACKNOWLEDGMENTS

I could never write a book without the help of my friends and my book community. Thank you Jet Tucker, Jamie Lewis, Diana Cormier, and Barbara Budan for taking the time to do the final reader proof. You can't imagine how much I appreciate it.

A huge thank you to Laura Moliter for her fantastic book editing.

Thank you to the fabulous Molly Phipps at wegotyoucoveredbookdesign.com for the beautiful book covers for the *Karass* series.

Thank you to every other member of my street team who helps me make so many decisions that help the book be the best book possible.

And always, thank you to my beloved husband, Del, for being my daily sounding board, for putting up with all my questions, my constant need to want to make things better, and for being the love of my life, in more than just this one lifetime.

ABOUT BECA LEWIS

Beca writes books that she hopes will change people's perceptions of themselves and the world, and open possibilities to things and ideas that are waiting to be seen and experienced.

At sixteen, Beca founded her own dance studio. Later, she received a Master's Degree in Dance in Choreography from UCLA and founded the Harbinger Dance Theatre, a multimedia dance company, while continuing to run her dance school.

After graduating—to better support her three children—Beca switched to the sales field, where she worked as an employee and independent contractor to many industries, excelling in each while perfecting and teaching her Shift® system, and writing books.

She joined the financial industry in 1983 and became an Associate Vice President of Investments at a major stock brokerage firm, and was a licensed Certified Financial Planner for more than twenty years.

This diversity, along with a variety of life challenges, helped fuel the desire to share what she's learned by writing and talking with the hope that it will make a difference in other people's lives.

Beca grew up in State College, PA, with the dream of becoming a dancer and then a writer. She carried that dream forward as she fulfilled a childhood wish by moving to Southern California in 1969. Beca told her family she would never move back to the cold.

After living there for thirty years, she met her husband Delbert Lee Piper, Sr., at a retreat in Virginia, and everything changed. They decided to find a place they could call their own which sent them off traveling around the United States. For a year or so they lived and worked in a few different places before returning to live in the cold once again near Del's family in a small town in Northeast Ohio, not too far from State College.

When not working and teaching together, they love to visit and play with their combined family of eight children and five grandchildren, read, study, do yoga or taiji, feed birds, work in their garden, and design things. Actually, designing things is what Beca loves to do. Del enjoys the end result.

CPSIA information can be obtained
at www.ICGtesting.com
Printed in the USA
LVHW081058030719
623093LV00003B/171/P

9 780971 952911